"I'll bet you never break the rules."

"I try not to," she said.

"You use the turn signal even when there aren't other cars behind you."

"Yes. And I tip twenty percent, even if the waitress is surly. I don't cheat on my taxes. Don't jaywalk. I follow the recipes exactly when I cook," she admitted.

"No risks. No adventures."

"I like order." She took a step toward him. Her voice softened to a whisper that made those solid values resonate with a purely sensual undertone. "I'm not a risk-taker. Sorry if that disappoints you."

His arm slipped around her slender waist and pulled her snug against him. "Who says I'm disappointed?"

He nuzzled her ear and felt her body respond with a quiver. At this moment, he wanted to give her all the stability her hear ____ ed.

She kissed him with a pa ____ ned at odds with her need f ____ wild. And he enjoyed ____ ted more.

Breaking awa ____ We should get back to the ____

To his bed.

CASSIE MILES

IN THE
MANOR
WITH THE
MILLIONAIRE

TORONTO • NEW YORK • LONDON
AMSTERDAM • PARIS • SYDNEY • HAMBURG
STOCKHOLM • ATHENS • TOKYO • MILAN • MADRID
PRAGUE • WARSAW • BUDAPEST • AUCKLAND

To Lee Carr, the world's greatest gothic writer.
And, as always, to Rick.

Special thanks and acknowledgment to Cassie Miles
for her contribution to The Curse of Raven's Cliff miniseries.

ISBN-13: 978-0-373-69341-2
ISBN-10:   0-373-69341-9

IN THE MANOR WITH THE MILLIONAIRE

ABOUT THE AUTHOR

For Cassie Miles, the best part about writing a story set in Eagle County near the Vail ski area is the ready-made excuse to head into the mountains for research. Though the winter snows are great for skiing, her favorite season is fall when the aspens turn gold.

The rest of the time, Cassie lives in Denver where she takes urban hikes around Cheesman Park, reads a ton and critiques often. Her current plans include a Vespa and a road trip, despite eye-rolling objections from her adult children.

Books by Cassie Miles

HARLEQUIN INTRIGUE

874—WARRIOR SPIRIT
904—UNDERCOVER COLORADO*
910—MURDER ON THE MOUNTAIN*
948—FOOTPRINTS IN THE SNOW
978—PROTECTIVE CONFINEMENT**
984—COMPROMISED SECURITY**
999—NAVAJO ECHOES
1025—CHRISTMAS COVER-UP
1048—MYSTERIOUS MILLIONAIRE
1074—IN THE MANOR WITH THE MILLIONAIRE

*Rocky Mountain Safe House
**Safe House: Mesa Verde

CAST OF CHARACTERS

Blake Monroe—This world-famous architect has been hired to oversee the renovations of Beacon Manor and the lighthouse. A widower, he still mourns the death of his wife, Kathleen.

Madeline Douglas—A proper schoolteacher from Boston, she's hired to be the live-in tutor for Blake's son. She comes to Raven's Cliff with secrets of her own.

Duncan Monroe—Blake's six-year-old son has been diagnosed with high-functioning autism.

Alma Eisen—The Beacon Manor housekeeper was once a foster mother for Madeline.

Dr. Teddy Fisher—The Beacon Manor owner whose scientific experiments might have caused an epidemic.

Helen Fisher—A librarian, this old maid resents the wealth of her brother, Teddy.

Perry Wells—Mayor of Raven's Cliff who lost his daughter on her wedding day.

Beatrice Wells—The Mayor's wife.

Grant Bridges—The ambitious Assistant District Attorney also coaches the local T-ball team.

Detective Andrei Lagios—Homicide investigator.

Sofia Lagios—Sister of Andrei, recently murdered by the Seaside Strangler.

Detective Joe Curtis—Newly transferred from the LAPD, he works with Lagios.

Alex Gibson—A local fisherman.

Marty Todd—Madeline's ne'er-do-well brother.

Chapter One

"One, two, three…" Duncan Monroe counted the steps as he climbed the stairs, not touching the banister or the wall. "…four, five, six."

That was how old he was. Six years old.

"Seven, eight, nine."

Here was where the staircase made a corner, and he could see to the top. Daddy had turned on the light in his bedroom, but there were shadows. Dark, scary shadows. Outside the rain came down and rattled against the windows.

Duncan shivered. Even though this was the middle of summertime, he felt cold on the inside. So cold it made his tummy hurt. Sometimes, when he touched people or things, he got creepy feelings like spider legs running up and down his arms. And he saw stuff. Bad stuff.

But he wasn't touching anything. His feet were in sneakers. He had on jeans and a long-sleeved T-shirt. He shouldn't be scared.

"Duncan." His dad called to him. "Are you getting ready for bed?"

"No." He hadn't meant to yell. His voice was too loud.

He covered his open mouth with both hands. His fingers pushed hard, holding back an even louder yell. His skin tasted like salt. Usually he wore gloves to keep from feeling things.

"Duncan, are you all right?"

His dad hated when Duncan was inappropriate. That's what his teacher used to call it. *Inappropriate behavior*. The doctors had other words for him. *Trauma. Autism. Hyper-something*. They all meant the same thing. He was a freak.

He yanked his hands down to his sides. "I'm okay."

"Get into your pajamas, buddy. I'll be there in a minute."

The shadow at the top of the stairs was as big as a T-Rex with giant, pointy teeth. Duncan wasn't going there. He turned around on the stairs and quietly counted backward. "Nine, eight, seven…"

He was at the front door of the big house they had just moved into. Though he didn't like touching doorknobs, he grabbed it and pulled.

Outside, the rain wasn't too bad. Big, fat drops splashed on the flat stones leading up to the front door. He stuck out his hand to catch them.

He walked out into it. Five steps. Then ten.

The light by the front door didn't reach very far into the dark. The thunder went boom. He heard the ocean smashing on the rocks at the bottom of the cliff.

He turned around and stared at the big house. On the first floor were four windows and one door, exactly in the middle. Five windows, all exactly the same size, on top. All exactly balanced. He liked that. What he didn't like was the big, old, wrecked-up tower that Daddy said used to be a lighthouse.

He looked toward it and saw a girl in a long dress and a red cape. She skipped toward the trees in the forest.

She giggled. Not the kind of mean laugh that kids used when they pointed at his gloves and called him Dunk the Skunk. She waved to him as though she wanted to play.

He heard her singing. "She sells seashells by the seashore."

MADELINE DOUGLAS gripped the steering wheel with both hands and squinted through her glasses at the narrow road winding through the thick Maine forest. Her headlights barely penetrated the rain and fog that had turned the summer night into a dense black shroud.

She opened her window to disperse the condensation on her windshield; the defroster in her ancient Volkswagen station wagon had quit working. This cranky old rattletrap always chose the worst possible moment to be temperamental. If the skies had been clear—the way normal weather in July ought to be—the defrost would have been fine.

How much farther? The man at the service station in Raven's Cliff where she'd spent her last ten bucks on gas told her that this road led to Beacon Manor. "Can't miss it," he'd said.

"We'll see about that," she muttered. Thus far, everything about her drive from Boston to this remote fishing village in Maine had gone wrong. An accident with a logging truck had clogged the highway. Then, she'd missed the turnoff and had to backtrack several miles. Then, her cell phone died. And now, the weather from hell.

At five minutes past eight o'clock, she was more than

half an hour late for her interview with world-famous architect Blake Monroe. Not to mention that she was a mess. Her green-patterned blouse didn't go with the bright red cardigan she'd dragged out of her suitcase when the rain started. Her khaki skirt was creased with wrinkles. Her black hair, pulled up in a knot on top of her head, had to be a frizz mop.

Somehow, she had to pull herself together and convince Blake Monroe to hire her as a tutor for his six-year-old son, Duncan, who had been diagnosed with a form of high-functioning autism. Though she had no formal training in handling kids with special needs, Madeline had been a substitute teacher for the past two years in Boston's inner-city schools. She had first-hand experience with a wide range of behaviors.

She'd convince him. *She had to.*

If Blake Monroe didn't hire her, she had a serious problem. With her meager supply of cash spent and her credit cards maxed, she couldn't even afford a cheap motel room for tonight. Sleeping in her car would be difficult; she'd crammed all her earthly belongings in here, including the potted ficus that sat beside her on the passenger seat.

The rain died down, replaced by gusts of fog that slapped against her windshield like tattered curtains. The tired old engine coughed on the verge of a breakdown as she emerged from the forest.

In the distance, perhaps a half mile away, she saw the glimmer of lights. Beacon Manor. Huge as a fortress, the mansion loomed in the foreboding darkness.

She maneuvered around a sharp curve that circled a stand of trees. On the opposite side, the shoulder of the road vanished into nothingness at the edge of a cliff. A dangerous precipice with no guard rail.

Her headlights shone on a dark-colored SUV parked smack in the middle of the road. His lights were off. There was no way around him.

She cranked the steering wheel hard left—away from the cliff—and slammed on the brake. Though she couldn't have been going more than twenty miles an hour, her tires skidded on the wet asphalt.

In slow motion, she saw the inevitable collision coming closer, inch by inch. Her brakes screeched. The fog whirled. Her headlights wavered.

Her right fender dinged the rear bumper of the SUV, and she jolted against her seat belt. Though the impact felt minor, the passenger-side airbag deployed against the ficus. Great! Her plant was protected from whiplash.

But not herself. The driver's-side airbag stayed in place. Like everything else in her life, it was broken.

She slumped over the steering wheel. A nasty, metallic stink from the engine gushed through her open window. A car wreck would have been disaster, and she ought to be grateful that her car wasn't a crumpled mass. Instead, hot tears burned the insides of her eyelids. In spite of a lifetime of careful plans and hard work, in spite of her best intentions...

A hand reached through the window and grabbed her upper arm. "What's wrong with you? Didn't you see me?"

Startled, she stared into the stark face of a smallish man with a goatee. A sheen of moisture accented the hollows beneath his eyes and his angry, distorted snarl.

He shook her. "Don't think you can run away. You'll pay for this damage."

Enough! She shoved open her door, forcing him back.

Justified rage shot through her as she leaped from the car into the drizzle. "You're the one at fault. Look where you're parked. There's no way I could get around you."

"You're trespassing." With his left hand, he pulled his collar tight around his throat. His right arm hung loosely at his side. "This is my property."

Her hopes sank. "Blake Monroe?"

"Monroe? He's the architect I hired to fix this place up." His skinny neck craned. Even so, he wasn't as tall as her own five feet, ten inches. "I own Beacon Manor. I'm Theodore Fisher. *Doctor* Fisher."

He announced himself as if she should be impressed, but she'd never heard of him. "All right, *Doctor*. Let's take a look at the damage."

The deep gouge on her fender blended with other scrapes and nicks. Dr. Fisher glanced at the scratch on his SUV, then turned his back on her. Clearly agitated, he walked wide of the two vehicles with tense, jerky steps. His brow furrowed as he peered into the darkness at the edge of the cliff. Watching for something? For someone? As he paced, he muttered under his breath. Though she couldn't make out the words, he sounded furious.

Madeline didn't want that crazy anger turned in her direction. Speaking with the measured voice she used to calm a classroom full of second-graders, she said, "We should exchange insurance information."

"Not necessary," he snapped.

"I agree." She wouldn't bother with this repair, couldn't afford to have her insurance premiums go up. "I'm willing to forget about this if you are."

His head swiveled on his neck. He focused intently on her. "Not trying to pull a fast one, are you?"

"Certainly not." She removed her rain-splattered glasses. His face blurred.

"Why are you here?" he demanded.

"I'm applying for a job as a tutor for Blake Monroe's son."

"So you'll be staying at the Manor. At my house." Very deliberately, he approached her. "I'll always know where to find you."

The wind wailed through the trees, and she heard something else. A voice? Dr. Fisher turned toward the sound. His arm raised. In his right hand, he held an automatic pistol.

SHE SELLS seashells…

In her long dress, she was the prettiest girl Duncan had ever seen. Her hair was golden. Her skin was white. She looked like the marble angel on Mama's gravestone.

"I would like to be your friend," she said. "My name is Temperance Raven."

"That's the name of this town," Duncan said. "Raven's Cliff."

"Named after my father," she said. "Captain Raven."

He knew she was telling a lie. The town was founded in 1794. He remembered that date, just as he remembered all numbers. So what if she fibbed? He liked the way she talked, like an accent. "Where are you from?"

"Dover in England."

They were standing under the trees, and his clothes were soppy. But she hardly seemed wet at all. "Come inside, Temperance. I'll show you my computer games."

Maybe he'd even let her win. Her smile was so pretty.

Seashells, seashells. By the seashore.

She held up her hand. "I brought a gift for you."

Before he could tell her that he never touched anyone or anything with his bare hands, she placed a glowing white shell on the ground before him. "It's for you, Duncan."

If he didn't pick it up, she'd think he was scared. Then she'd laugh at him and run away. So, he leaned down and grabbed the shell. It burned his hand. He couldn't let go. Shivers ran up his arm. There was a roar inside his head.

"Temperance." He gasped.

"I am here, Duncan. I will always be here for you."

His eyes closed and he fell to the ground. In his mind, he saw a whole different place. A different time: Sunset. He was at the bottom of the cliff, near the rocks that stuck out into the waves.

He moaned and tried to get up. Something very bad had happened in this place and time, something that had to do with the shell....

He saw a pretty lady with curly black hair. Sofia, her name was Sofia. She had on a long white dress, kind of like the one Temperance wore, and she was lying on the rocks. Duncan felt her fear. Inside his head, he heard her silent screams for help, but she was too weak to move. Couldn't even lift a finger.

Someone else chanted. In a low voice, he sang about the sea. The dangers of the sea. The curse of the sea.

Duncan couldn't see his face. But he knew. This man was very bad. Very strong. Very mean. He put a necklace of seashells over Sofia's head.

"No," Duncan cried out. "Stop him. No."

The bad man pulled the necklace tighter and tighter. He twisted hard. Duncan felt the shells bite into his own throat. He couldn't breathe.

Lying on the wet grasses, he shook and shook. He was crying. He heard grunts and whimpers, and he knew the sounds were coming from him.

His eyes opened.

There was a lady kneeling beside him. She wore glasses. Her hair was pulled back, but some had got loose. It was black and curly. She looked kind of like Sofia. He whispered the name. "Sofia?"

"My name is Madeline," she said, reaching toward him. "Are you—"

"Don't," he yelled. "Don't touch me. Never touch."

She held up both hands. "Okay. Whatever you say. You're Duncan, right?"

He sat up and looked around for Temperance. She was gone. But he still held the shell in his hand. It was a warning. Temperance had warned him about the bad man.

He scrambled to his feet. Where was Temperance? Where was his friend? "She sells seashells…"

"By the seashore." The lady smiled and stood beside him. She was tall for a girl. "She sells seashells."

"By the seashore," he said.

She pointed. "Do you see that light over there? I'll bet that's your father's flashlight."

"He's going to be mad. I was inappropriate."

Madeline looked down at the sopping-wet boy in his jeans and T-shirt. A terrible sadness emanated from this child. She longed to cuddle him in her arms and reassure him, but she'd promised not to touch.

"There's nothing wrong with being inappropriate," she said. "I've often been that way myself."

He stared up at her. "Are you a freak?"

"Absolutely." She took off her glasses, tried wiping the

lenses on her damp shirt and gave up, stowing them in the pocket of her skirt. "It takes someone courageous to be different. I think you're very brave, Duncan."

The hint of a smile curved his mouth. "You do?"

"Very brave indeed." She bobbed her head. "Let's find your father."

When the boy took off running toward the flashlight's beacon, Madeline had a hard time keeping up. The two-inch heels on the beige leather pumps she'd worn to create a professional appearance for her interview made divots in the rain-soaked earth.

The flashlight's beam wavered, then charged in their direction. In seconds, a tall man in a hooded rain poncho was upon them. He held out his arms to Duncan, but the boy stopped a few yards away and folded his arms across his skinny torso. "I'm okay, Daddy."

"Thank God," his father murmured. "I was worried."

"I'm okay," Duncan shouted.

Blake Monroe dropped to one knee. He reached toward his son. Without touching the boy, he caressed the air around him with such poignancy that Madeline's heart ached.

Before she'd set out on this journey, she'd taken a couple of minutes to check out Blake Monroe on the Internet. An internationally renowned architect and designer, he'd worked in Berlin, Paris and all over the United States, most notably on historic renovations and exclusive boutique hotels. His international fame was somewhat intimidating, but right now he was a frightened parent whose only concern was the safety of his child.

Blake stood, whipped off his poncho and dropped it around his son's shoulders.

When he turned toward her, a flash of lightning illuminated his high cheekbones and the sharp line of his jaw. Even without her glasses, she realized that he was one of the most handsome men she'd ever seen.

The rain started up with renewed fury, lashing against his broad shoulders, but he didn't cower the way she did. His powerful presence suggested a strength that could match the raging storm. His fiery gaze met her eyes, and a sizzle penetrated her cold, wet body.

"Who are you?"

"Madeline Douglas. I'm here about the teaching position."

"What were you doing out here with my son?"

There was an unmistakable accusation in his question. He blamed her? Did he think she'd lured Duncan out of the house in this storm?

Fumbling in her pocket, she found her glasses and stuck them onto her nose, wishing she had a ten-inch-thick shield of bulletproof glass to protect herself from his hostility. "I was driving along the road, just coming out of the forest. And I had a bit of an accident with Dr. Fisher."

"The owner of the Manor," Blake said. "Nice move."

Though Madeline had done nothing wrong, she felt defensive. "We decided that the damage was too minor to report. Then we heard something from the forest. Voices." With Duncan standing here, she decided not to mention Dr. Fisher's gun. "I followed the sound of Duncan's voice. Found him at the edge of the trees."

"She did," Duncan said. "She's pretty. I thought she was Sofia."

Blake tensed. He hunkered down so his eyes were level with his son's. "What name did you say?"

"Poor, poor Sofia. She's with Mama and the angels."

"Did you see something, Duncan?"

"No," he shouted. "No, no, no."

"Let's go inside," Blake said.

Duncan spun in a circle. "Where's Temperance? She's my friend."

"Time for bed, son. Back to the house. You can count the steps."

The boy walked toward the front door in a perfectly straight line, counting each step aloud.

Without saying another word to her, Blake walked beside him.

"Hey," she called after them. "Should I bring my car around to the front?"

"I don't give a damn what you do."

A scream of sheer frustration crawled up the back of her throat. This trip was cursed. Every instinct warned her to give up, to turn back, find another way.

But she was desperate.

Through the driving rain, she heard Duncan counting and singing. "She sells seashells…"

Chapter Two

Gathering up the remnants of her shredded self-respect, Madeline chased after Blake and his son. If she didn't follow them into the house, she was certain that the door would be locked against her. Not only did she need this job, but she wanted it. She'd connected with Duncan. In him, she saw a reflection of her own childhood. She knew what it was like to be called a freak. Always to be an outsider.

As the daughter of a drug-addicted mother and an absent father, she'd been shuffled from one foster home to another until she was finally adopted by the Douglases when she was twelve. In spite of their kindness and warmth, Madeline still hadn't fitted in with other kids. Her adopted family was poor, and she grew too fast. Her secondhand clothing never fitted properly on her long, gangly frame. And then there were the glasses she'd worn since first grade.

Most of the time, her childhood was best forgotten. But, oddly, her past had brought her here. Standing in the doorway of Beacon Manor, Madeline saw someone she had once lived with. Alma Eisen.

Eighteen years ago, Alma had been a foster parent for Madeline and her older brother, Marty. They'd stayed with her for a year—a dark and terrible year during which Alma had decided to divorce her abusive husband. Unlike the other fosters, Alma had stayed in touch with Christmas cards and birthday greetings, which Madeline had dutifully responded to.

It was Alma—now employed as Blake's housekeeper and cook—who had told Madeline about the tutoring position. At the door to the manor, she greeted Madeline with a smile but held her at arm's length, not wanting to get wet. "What on earth happened to you?"

"Long story."

The years had been kind to Alma Eisen. Her hair was still blond and elaborately styled with spit curls at the cheeks. Her makeup, including blue eye shadow, almost disguised the wrinkles. Madeline figured that this petite woman had to be in her fifties. "You look terrific."

"Thanks, hon. Wish I could say the same for you."

Blake had followed his son—who was still counting aloud—to the top of the staircase.

Madeline called to him. "Mr. Monroe?"

He glared. "What is it?"

"I came all this way, sir. At the very least, I'd like to have an interview."

"After I get my son to bed, I'll deal with you."

He turned away. Though Madeline wasn't a betting woman, she guessed that her odds of being hired were about a thousand to one. A shiver trembled through her.

"You need to get out of those wet clothes," Alma said, "before you catch your death of cold."

"I don't have anything to change into. My car is parked way down the road."

"Come with me, hon. I'll take care of you."

Though Alma had stayed in touch, Madeline didn't remember her as a particularly nurturing woman. Her phone call about this job had been a huge surprise, and Madeline couldn't help wondering about Alma's motives. What could she hope to gain from having Madeline working here?

She trailed the small woman up the grand staircase and looked back down at the graceful oval of the foyer. She couldn't see into any of the other rooms. Doors were closed, and plastic sheeting hung across the arched entry to what must have been a drawing room. Signs of disrepair marred the grandeur of the manor, but the design showed a certain civility and elegance, like a dowager duchess who had fallen on hard times.

Alma hustled her past Duncan's bedroom to the far end of the long, wainscoted hallway with wallpaper peeling in the corners. She opened the door farthest from the staircase and hustled Madeline inside.

The center light reflected off the crystals of a delicate little chandelier. With dark wood furnishings, somewhat worn, and a four-poster bed with a faded gray silk duvet, this bedroom was the essence of "shabby chic."

"Guest room," Alma said as she rummaged through the drawers of a bureau. "This is where you'll be staying after you're hired."

"Hired?" She scoffed. "I doubt it. Blake Monroe can't stand me."

"In any case, you're staying here tonight. It's not safe for you to be out." She tossed a pair of sweatpants and a T-shirt toward her. "These ought to fit. They were left behind by one of Blake's friends who spent the night."

Madeline picked up the ratty gray sweatpants. "I really appreciate this, Alma."

"Don't thank me yet." She lowered her voice. "This little town, Raven's Cliff, comes with a curse."

"Superstitions," Madeline said.

"Don't be so sure. There's a serial killer on the loose. A couple of weeks ago, he murdered two girls on the eve of their senior prom. One of them was the sister of a local cop. Sofia Lagios."

Sofia. Duncan had looked at Madeline and spoken that name. "What did she look like?"

"I've only seen photographs. But she was a bit like you. Long, curly black hair."

Duncan must have heard people talking about the serial killer. But why would a six-year-old remember the name of a murder victim?

"Get changed," Alma said. "I'll tell Blake that you're too pooped to talk tonight. In the morning, you can have a nice, professional interview."

"Great." She dropped her car keys on top of the bureau. "Nothing sounds better right now than a good night's sleep."

BLAKE LINGERED in the doorway of his son's bedroom, gazing with all the love he possessed at Duncan's angelic little face. So beautiful. So like his mother. Often, when Blake looked into his son's bright blue eyes, he saw Kathleen staring back at him. On those rare occasions when Duncan laughed, he heard echoes of her own joy, and he remembered the good times. Only three years ago, cancer had taken her away from him forever.

"Time for sleep, Duncan."

As usual, no response.

To get an answer, Blake used the rhyming repetition that his son enjoyed. "Nighty-night. Sleep tight…"

"And don't let the bedbugs bite," Duncan said.

Sometimes, the kid scared the hell out of him. Tonight, when he'd disappeared, Blake had feared disaster. A fall from the precipitous cliffs near the lighthouse. An attack by wild dogs or animals. Worse, a confrontation with a serial killer. Why had Duncan spoken the name of one of the victims? The boy must have known that Sofia Lagios was dead because he said she was with the angels. But how? How had he known?

Life would be a lot easier if Blake could ask a simple question and get a simple answer, but his son's brain didn't work that way.

Duncan stared up at the fluorescent stars Blake had attached to the ceiling in a precise geometric pattern. "I have a friend," he said. "She sells seashells."

"That's great, buddy." It had to be an imaginary friend. He hadn't been around any other children. "What's her name?"

"Temperance Raven. She wears a red cape." His tiny fingers laced together, then pulled apart. He repeated the action three times. "I like French fries."

"Where did you meet Temperance?"

"By the lighthouse. She wanted me to play with her."

Blake didn't like the sound of this. The lighthouse was under construction, dangerous. "Was Temperance outside? In the rain?"

Duncan turned to his side. "Seashells, seashells, sea-shells…"

"Goodnight, son."

Blake left the door to his son's bedroom ajar. Duncan wanted it that way.

Blake wanted to find out what had happened tonight,

and there was one person who could tell him. He'd seen Alma escorting that very wet young woman down the hall toward the guest room. What was her name? Madeline? She might be able to give him information about Duncan's supposed new friend. Blake tapped on her door.

"Alma?" she called out. "Come on in."

Blake strode inside. "We need to talk."

Wearing baggy sweatpants and an oversize T-shirt, she stood in front of the mirror above the antique dressing table. Her long black hair fell past her shoulders in a mass of damp tangles. As soon as she spotted him, she grabbed her black-framed glasses and stuck them on the end of her straight, patrician nose. "Mr. Monroe. I thought we might have our interview tomorrow."

He'd almost forgotten that she was here to apply for a job as his son's tutor. "I need to know what happened tonight. Duncan mentioned someone named Temperance."

"I didn't see anyone else," she said. "There aren't any other houses nearby, are there?"

"We're isolated."

"That could be a problem." She pushed the heavy mane away from her face. Her complexion was fresh, with rosy tints on her cheeks and the tip of her nose. Behind those glasses, black lashes outlined her eyes. An unusual color. Aquamarine.

"Problem?" he asked.

"Not having neighbors." She gave him a prim smile. "Surely, you'll want Duncan to have playmates."

"He doesn't do well with other children."

"I know," she said. "He told me."

Like hell he did. His son's conversations were limited to discussions of simple activities, like brushing his teeth. Or repetitions. Or numbers.

She continued, "He was worried that you'd be angry because he was…how did he say it? Inappropriate."

That sounded like Duncan. "His teachers said his behavior was inappropriate. The word stuck in his mind."

"Everybody's like that. We all tend to remember the words that hurt. To let criticism soak in."

His son wasn't like everybody else. Far from it. But he appreciated the way she phrased her comments, and Duncan seemed to like her. Maybe Madeline Douglas would be a suitable tutor, after all.

He crossed the room and took a seat in a carved wooden rocking chair, one of several handmade pieces in the manor. "Show me your résumé and recommendations."

When she gestured toward the window, the graceful motion of her wrist contrasted the baggy black T-shirt. "All my papers are in my car, which is still down the road."

"Where you ran into Teddy Fisher."

"I didn't want to mention this in front of Duncan," she said, "but Dr. Fisher had a handgun."

Not good news. He hated to hear that the local loons were armed. Fisher had tons of money and a decent reputation as a scientist with his own laboratories in Raven's Cliff. He came from a good family; his father had been a Nobel Prize winner. But Teddy's behavior went beyond eccentric into borderline insanity.

The main reason Blake had taken this job—a step down from his typically high-profile architectural assignments— was because he wanted to get Duncan out of the city into a small-town environment where the pace was slow and distractions were minimal.

"Teddy Fisher owns the Manor," he said. "But he's not supposed to visit without notifying me. I'll remind him."

She gave a brisk nod. "If you like, I can tell you about my qualifications."

"Do it."

She started by rattling off her educational achievements, special recognitions and a bachelor's degree from an undistinguished college which had taken six years because she'd been holding down a job while going to school. For two years, she'd taught second grade at a parochial school. "Then I started substitute teaching in some of Boston's inner-city schools."

He held up his hand, signaling a stop. "Why did you leave a full-time position to be a sub?"

"Alma might have mentioned that I grew up in the foster-care system."

Vaguely, he recalled some comment. "She might have."

"I was a throwaway kid. No one expected me to amount to much. But I had a teacher in third grade…a wonderful teacher. She wouldn't let me shirk on my assignments, made me work hard and kept after me to do better. She noticed me."

Behind her glasses, her eyes teared up. "She changed my life. By working in inner-city schools, I felt like I might make that kind of difference."

He liked her earnest compassion. She sure as hell had the empathy needed to work with his son. But did she have the training? Blake wasn't accustomed to settling for second best. "How much do you know about autism?"

She picked up a straight-back wooden chair and moved it close to his rocker. When she sat, she leaned forward. "What can you tell me about Duncan's behavior?"

"On the behavioral range of autism, he's considered to be high-functioning." Blake had taken his son to a cadre of doctors and therapists. "Initially, we tried drug therapy, but Duncan didn't respond well. The specialists call his condition a form of hypersensitivity."

"Which is why he doesn't like to be touched."

"When he touches someone, he says that he knows what they're thinking."

"Like a psychic."

"Don't go there," he warned. It was difficult enough to manage Duncan's illness without the extra burden of some harebrained, paranormal philosophy.

"I'm trying to understand," she said. "When I found Duncan in the woods, we had a coherent communication. More important, he reacted to me. He looked me in the eye, and he smiled. That behavior isn't consistent with what I know about autism."

Her presumption ticked him off. For the past three years, since his wife had died, he'd struggled with his son's condition. They'd gone through brain scans, blood tests, physical and psychological diagnostics…. He rose from the rocking chair. "Are you an expert?"

"No, but I can see the obvious." Instead of cowering, she stood to confront him. "Duncan is smart. And he cares about what you think. He wants you to love him."

Her words were a slap in the face. Tight-lipped, he said, "This interview is over."

WITH THE ECHO of the door slamming behind Blake still ringing in her ears, Madeline collapsed onto the bed. Disaster! She'd infuriated Blake and blown her chance at this job. Truly a shame because she thought she might work well with Duncan, and she found herself drawn to his father. What red-blooded woman wouldn't be? Blake was gorgeous and intense. Unfortunately, he despised her.

She shifted around on the bed. Before she went to sleep, she needed to use the facilities.

Since there was no adjoining bathroom with this bedroom, she had to go into the hallway. Poking her head out the door, she checked to make sure Blake was nowhere in sight. One doorway stood ajar and light spilled into the corridor. Duncan's room. She tiptoed past.

"Madeline?"

Peeking into his room, she said, "You remembered my name. Hi, Duncan."

"Will I see my friend again?"

She had no right to be here, no justifiable reason to talk with Blake's son. But she couldn't turn away from this troubled child. Slipping into his room, she pulled a rocking chair near his bed. "Is her name Temperance?"

"Temperance Raven."

"Like the town," Madeline said. "Raven's Cliff."

"Temperance lied to me about the town being named after her daddy in 1794. But I don't care. Lots of people lie. Liar, liar, pants on fire."

"Hang them up on a telephone wire," she responded. "You like rhymes."

"Temperance gave me a present." He rolled over on his bed and picked up a smooth, white shell.

Madeline grinned. "She sells seashells."

"By the seashore," Duncan concluded.

Though their conversation scattered in several directions, they were communicating. Instead of telling him that she liked his room, she pointed up at the ceiling and recited, "Starlight, star bright. First star I see tonight."

He watched her with an intensity that reminded her of his father. "Finish the rhyme."

"Wish I may, wish I might, have the wish I wish tonight."

He parroted the rhyme back to her perfectly. Not once, but three times. Then he laughed.

Hearing a sound near the door, she glanced over her shoulder and saw Blake standing in the hallway. He stepped away too quickly for her to decide if he was angry about her talking to Duncan. And, frankly, she didn't care. This wasn't about him.

"Duncan," she said, "I know a very long rhyme. A poem about baseball."

He nodded for her to continue.

"You'd like baseball. It's all about numbers." She drew a diamond in the air as she talked about the bases and the pitcher and the batter. "Four balls and three strikes."

"Three strikes and you're out," he said.

"You're right," she said. "This poem is called 'Casey at the Bat.'"

He lay back on his pillow to listen while she recited the poem she'd memorized in fifth grade. The rhyming cadence lulled him, and Duncan's eyelids began to droop.

When she had finished, he roused himself. "Again."

She started over. By the time she finished, he was sound asleep.

Leaving his door ajar, exactly the way she'd found it, she went down the hallway to the bathroom. Like every other part of the house she'd seen, the room was sorely in need of fresh paint. But it seemed clean and had an old-fashioned claw-footed tub. Fantastic! One of her favorite pastimes was a long, hot soak. And why not? It wasn't as if she could make Blake Monroe dislike her even more. Besides, she didn't know when or if she'd ever have the chance to luxuriate in a tub again.

As she filled the tub, fears about her uncertain future arose. No money. No job. No home. She had only enough gas to get back to Raven's Cliff. That would have to be where she started her new life, maybe working as a waitress or a short-order cook. She had experience at both from when she was putting herself through college.

Stripping off the sweatpants and T-shirt, she eased into the hot, steamy water.

Damn it, Marty. This is all your fault. Her brother had popped back into her life just long enough to wreck everything. When he'd showed up, she should have thrown him out on his handsome butt. Should have, but didn't. Water under the bridge.

After a nice, long soak, she climbed out of the tub, somewhat refreshed, and padded down the hallway to her "shabby chic" room.

The door was open, just the way she'd left it. But something was different. At the foot of her bed was the canvas suitcase that had been in the back of her car. Had Alma trudged all the way down the road to get it? She opened the flap and took out a nightgown.

"Madeline Douglas."

She turned and saw Blake standing in the doorway. He tossed the keys to her car to the center of the bed. "You shouldn't leave these lying around."

"I didn't." The keys had been on top of the bureau in her room. *Inside her room!* Even if the door was open, he shouldn't have barged in uninvited.

"You're hired," he said without smiling. "We'll talk in the morning."

The door closed behind him.

Chapter Three

The next morning, the skies outside Madeline's bedroom window were clear, washed clean by the rain. And she tried to focus on the sunny side. She had a job and a place to live. Working with Duncan provided an interesting challenge. For now, she was safe.

The dark cloud on her emotional horizon was Blake Monroe. A volatile man. She didn't know why he had changed his mind about hiring her and decided it was best not to ask too many questions. He didn't seem like the type of man who bothered to explain himself.

Entering the high-ceilinged kitchen, she smiled at Alma, who sat at the table, drinking coffee and keeping company with a morning television chat program on a small flat-screen.

"I'm hired," Madeline announced. "I can't thank you enough for telling me about this job."

"Congrats." Using the remote, Alma turned down the volume. "How about lending me a hand with breakfast?"

"Sure."

She turned and confronted a mountain of dirty dishes, glasses, pots and crusted skillets that spread across the countertop like a culinary apocalypse. It appeared that Alma hadn't wiped a single plate since they'd moved into this house.

How could anyone stand such a mess! Madeline rolled up the sleeves of her daisy-patterned cotton shirt, grabbed an apron that was wadded in the corner of the counter and dug in.

"You haven't changed a bit," Alma said. "Even as a kid, you were good about cleaning up."

Maybe even a teensy bit compulsive. "Is that why you thought of me for this job?"

"I don't mind having a helper." Alma shuffled toward the butcher-block island and leaned against it. Though she was completely dressed with hair and makeup done, she wore fuzzy pink slippers. "Did you sleep well?"

"Took me a while to get accustomed to the creaks and groans in this old house." Once during the night, she'd startled awake, certain that someone had been in the room with her. She'd even imagined that she saw the door closing, which made her wonder. "Does Duncan ever sleepwalk?"

"Not as far as I know, but I wouldn't be surprised by anything that kid does. Or his father, for that matter."

"Is Blake difficult to work for?"

"A real pain in the rear."

Yet, he put up with the mess in the kitchen. "How so?"

"In the past year, he went through two other housekeepers and four nannies."

"Why?"

"His lordship is one of those dark, brooding, artistic types. Real moody. Gets caught up in a project and nothing else matters. He forgets to eat, then blames you for not feeding him." She patted her sculpted blond curls. "It's not part of my job description to keep track of his phone calls, and most of the business contacts go through his office in New York. But if I forget a phone call, he blows a gasket."

"He yells at you?" Madeline was beginning to feel more and more trepidation about this job.

"Never raises his voice," Alma said. "He growls. Real low. Like an angry lion."

With Blake's overgrown dark blond mane and intense hazel eyes, a lion was an apt comparison. As Madeline rinsed glasses and loaded them into the dishwasher, she said, "I looked Blake up on the Internet. He does amazing restorations. There were interior photos of this gorgeous hotel in Paris."

"Paris." Alma sighed. "That's what I expected when I signed on as a housekeeper four months ago. Trips to Europe. Fancy places. Fancy people. La-di-dah."

"Sounds like a lovely adventure."

"So far, I've been at the brownstone in Manhattan and here—Maine. I mean, Maine? The whole state is about as glamorous as a lumberjack's plaid shirt." She paused to sip her coffee. "Let's hear about you, hon. How's your big brother, Marty?"

At the mention of her brother's name, Madeline almost dropped the plate she was scrubbing in the sink. "We've kind of lost touch."

"Good-looking kid. A bit devilish, though. Didn't he get into some kind of trouble with the law?"

She heard Duncan counting his steps as he came down the hall to the kitchen and assumed his father wasn't far behind. "I'd rather not talk about Marty."

"It's okay." Alma patted her arm. "I won't say a word."

Duncan preceded his father into the kitchen. His clothing was the same as last night: a long-sleeved, striped T-shirt and jeans. At the table, he climbed into his chair and sat, staring straight ahead.

Alma went into action. She measured oat-bran cereal into a clear glass bowl, then measured the milk. She placed them in front of Duncan, then fetched a pre-chilled glass of OJ from the fridge.

Neither she nor Blake said a word.

Madeline assumed this was some sort of ritual and didn't interfere until Duncan had taken his first bite of cereal. Then she took a seat opposite him and watched as he chewed carefully before swallowing. She smiled. "Good morning, Duncan."

He said nothing, didn't acknowledge her presence in any way.

Blake cleared his throat. When she looked at him, he shook his head, warning her not to rock the boat. She rose from her seat and went toward him. Seeing him in the morning light, she noticed the lightly etched crow's feet at the corners of his eyes and the unshaven stubble on his chin. He dragged his fingers through his unruly dark blond hair. His careless grooming and apparent disarray reminded her of an unmade bed that had been torn apart in a night of wild, sexual abandon.

She intended to discuss her plans for Duncan's lessons. After his interest in the "Casey at the Bat" poem, she'd decided to use baseball as a learning tool. There were other things she needed to ask Blake about, such as her salary, rules of the household and teaching supplies. But being near him left her tongue-tied.

She pushed her glasses up on her nose and said, "Do you have a baseball?"

"I can find one."

Her cheeks were warm with embarrassment. Seldom was she so inarticulate. "Other supplies? Pencils and paper?"

"Everything you'll need is in a room at the end of this hallway. It was once a conservatory so there's a whole wall of windows. Until the renovations are done, we're using it as a family room. Alma can show you."

She stammered. "I-is there, um, some kind of schedule?"

He lifted an eyebrow; his expression changed from arrogant to vaguely amused. He stretched out his arm and pointed to the wall beside her. "How's this?"

Right in front of her nose was a three-foot-by-two-foot poster board with a heading in letters five inches high: Duncan's Schedule. The entire day was plotted in detail.

"I've found," he said, "that Duncan does best when we stick to a consistent routine."

She pointed to the slot after breakfast. "Quiet Time in Family Room. What does that mean?"

"Exactly what it says. Duncan likes to spend time by himself, and all his toys are in the family room. Usually he plays computer games."

The next slot said Lessons. "How do I know where to start?"

"Duncan's last tutor left a log that detailed her teaching plans and Duncan's progress. She wasn't a live-in, and I can't say that I was happy with her results." He glanced toward the housekeeper. "Is that coffee hot?"

"Piping."

He went to the coffeemaker and filled a mug. "Well, Alma, it's nice to see that you're finally cleaning up in here."

"I aim to please," she said. "Breakfast in your studio?"

"Eggs over easy, wheat toast and bacon."

With a nod to Madeline, he left the kitchen.

Though his back was turned, she made a "bye-bye" motion with her hand. Oh, good grief. Could she possibly be more of a dork?

Alma chuckled. "Got a little crush on his lordship?"

"Of course not."

"He's a handsome thing. And he's even taller than you are. Probably six foot two or three."

"I hadn't noticed."

She returned to the sink and dug into the stack of dirty dishes with renewed vigor. After she'd cleaned up the kitchen and grabbed an energy bar for breakfast, she trailed Duncan into the family room. He spoke not a word, went directly to his computer and turned it on.

Like the kitchen, this room was a mess. Sunlight gushed through a wall of windows, illuminating a cluttered worktable where Duncan sat at his computer. Though the wall had a neat row of storage bins and shelves, everything had been heaped on the floor—played with and then discarded.

The chaos didn't make sense. Every hour of Duncan's day was regimented, but here—in the place where he was supposed to learn—he was surrounded by disarray.

Obviously, she needed to put things in order. One of the earliest lessons taught in grade school was "Putting Things Away." Getting Duncan to participate in the clean-up would have been good, but she didn't want to disrupt his schedule. This hour was for quiet time.

While he fiddled with his computer, she picked up a plush blue pony and placed it on the shelf labeled Stuffed Animals. Then another stuffed toy. Blocks in the bin.

Crayons back in their box. Trucks and cars on another labeled shelf.

Eventually, she found a place for everything. "All done," she said. "I'm going out to my car to bring a few things inside."

He didn't even glance in her direction. No communication whatsoever. A cone of isolation surrounded him. No one was allowed to touch.

After running up to her bedroom to grab her car keys, she stepped outside into the sunny warmth of a July day. Her beat-up Volkswagen station wagon with the brand-new dent from her collision with Dr. Fisher was parked just outside the front door. When she unlocked the back, she noticed that the flaps on a couple of boxes were open. She hadn't put them in here like that. Everything had been sealed with tape or had the flaps tucked in. Had someone been tampering with her things? When Blake got her suitcase, did he also search her belongings?

Before she built up a full-blown anger at him about his callous intrusion into her privacy, a more ominous thought occurred. What if it was someone else?

Last night, she'd sensed that someone was in her bedroom. She hadn't actually seen anyone; it was just a fleeting impression. But what if it were true? Dr. Fisher had said that he'd "always know where to find her." He owned this house. Surely he had a key. But why would he look through her things?

"Need some help?" Alma called from the doorway.

Madeline slammed the rear door. "I'll worry about this stuff later. But I need to get the ficus out of the front seat before it wilts."

She unlocked the passenger-side door and liberated

the plant. The ficus itself wasn't anything special, but the fluted porcelain pot painted with rosebuds was one of her favorite things.

"Heavy," she muttered as she kicked the car door closed and lurched toward the house, not stopping until she reached her second-floor bedroom where she set the plant near the window. The delicately painted pot looked as though it belonged here—more than she did.

Had someone crept into her room last night? There was no way to prove she'd had an intruder unless she contacted the police and had them take fingerprints. Even then, Dr. Fisher had a right to be in the house; he owned the place. If not Fisher, who? The serial killer. His last victim, Sofia, had looked like her.

Madeline plucked off her glasses and wiped the lenses. She didn't want to raise an alarm about a prowler unless she had tangible evidence. Tonight, before she went to bed, she'd push the ficus against the door so no one could enter without making a lot of noise.

She hurried down the staircase toward the family room. In the doorway, she came to an abrupt halt. The room she had so carefully cleaned was ransacked. Stuffed animals had been flung in every direction. Books spilled across the floor. The toy trucks and cars looked like a major highway collision. Little Duncan stood in the midst of it, oblivious to her presence.

Either she could laugh or cry. She chose the former, letting out her frustration in a chuckle. Now she knew why the room had been a mess.

Duncan paced toward her. When he held out his hand, she saw that he was wearing latex gloves. In the center of his palm was the white seashell he'd shown her last night.

"Temperance," she said.

He marched past her into the corridor that led to the front door. His clear intention was to go outside. And how could she stop him? From the information she had on autistic kids, she knew that corporal punishment often led to tantrums. Arguments were futile.

The key, she decided, was to gain his trust. Maybe she could impart a few bits of knowledge along the way.

At the front door, she stepped ahead of him, blocking his way and creating the illusion that she was in control. "We're going to take a walk. Across the yard to the forest. And we'll gather pinecones. Six pinecones."

"Ten," he said.

"Ten is good."

Outside, he started counting his steps. "One, two, three…"

"*Uno, dos, tres.* Those are Spanish numbers."

He repeated the words back to her. She took him up to ten in Spanish, then started over. At least he was learning something.

Halfway across the grassy stretch leading to the forested area, Blake jogged up beside them.

"It's such a beautiful day," she said. "We decided to do our lesson outdoors."

"Couldn't stand the mess in the family room?"

"I might be a bit of a neat freak," she admitted. "Anyway, we're learning numbers in Spanish."

He fell into step beside her, and she surreptitiously peeked up at him. Definitely taller than she, he moved with a casual, athletic grace.

Near the woods, Duncan scampered ahead of them.

"It's good for him to be outside," Blake said. "Gives him a chance to work on his coordination."

"His fine motor skills are okay. He didn't seem to be having any problem with the computer."

"It's the big stuff that gives him problems. Running, skipping, playing catch."

Duncan had entered the trees but was still clearly visible. She glanced over her shoulder at the house. In daylight, the two-story, beige-brick building with four tall chimneys looked elegant and imposing. "What are your plans for the Manor?"

He was taken aback by her question. "How much do you know about historic restoration?"

"Very little. But I looked up some of your other architectural projects on the Web. Many seemed more modern than traditional."

"That's one reason why this project appealed to me. I plan to restore the American Federalist style while totally updating with new wiring, plumbing and insulation. I want to go green—make it ecological."

"Solar panels?"

"Too clumsy," he said. "The challenge in this project," he said, "is to maintain the original exterior design and restore the decorative flourishes of the interior. At the same time, I'm planning modern upgrades. Maybe a sauna and gym in the basement."

As he talked about architecture, she caught a glimpse of a different Blake Monroe—a man who was passionate about his work. Still intense, but focused. And eager to have an adult conversation.

She liked this side of his personality. Liked him a lot.

"SHE SELLS SEASHELLS…" Duncan repeated the rhyme again and again. "Temperance, where are you?"

"Here I am."

She stood with her back against a tree. He could see her, but his daddy and Madeline couldn't. And that was good. He didn't want to share his new friend.

He held out the shell. "You gave me this to warn me about the bad man."

She bent down and picked up a pinecone. Her shiny golden hair fell across her face. "There is something dangerous in the Manor."

"What?"

"Perhaps the basement. I cannot enter the Manor."

"You don't have to be scared, Temperance. I won't let anybody hurt you."

She placed a pinecone into his gloved hand. "You need ten of these. For your teacher."

He was happy to have a friend who didn't tease about his gloves. "I'm very brave. Madeline said so."

"Duncan, you must not forget the danger."

"Danger," he repeated.

Chapter Four

Half an hour before the scheduled time for lunch, Madeline was pleased with their progress. She and Duncan had arranged the ten pinecones for an afternoon art project. And they'd read an entire book about trains.

Her initial assessment of his skills matched the reports from his previous tutor. Exceptional mathematic ability. Reading and writing skills were poor.

Duncan jumped to his feet. "I want to explore."

"So do I," she said. "We could get your father to give us a tour. He knows a lot about the Manor."

"No," he shouted. "No."

His loud, strident voice had an edge to it. She hadn't figured out how to deal with disagreements, but it couldn't be good to continually back down to his demands. She replied with a statement, not a question. "We'll explore one room."

"Basement," he said.

Not what she was hoping for. She should have been more specific, should have told him that they would explore his father's studio, which would give her a chance to spend a bit more time with Blake. Unfortunately, she hadn't specified a room, and she needed to be unambiguous with Duncan. "The basement it is."

The door leading to the basement was off the kitchen where Alma should have been preparing lunch. She was nowhere in sight.

Madeline turned on the light, revealing a wooden staircase that descended straight down. "I'll go first," she said. "You need to hold tight to the railing."

Duncan followed behind her, counting each step aloud.

A series of bare bulbs lit the huge space that was divided with heavy support pillars and walls. The ceiling was only eight feet high. Like most unfinished basements, it was used for storage. There were stacks of old boxes, discarded furniture and tools. A series of notched shelves suggested that the basement had at one time been a wine cellar.

A damp, musty smell coiled around them, and she shuddered, thinking of rats and spiders. As far as she could tell, there were no windows.

"I've seen enough," she said.

Duncan reached out and touched a concrete wall with his gloved hand. "Danger," he said.

The word startled her.

He zigzagged from the walls to the stairs and back. In spite of her rising trepidation, Madeline noticed a geometric pattern in his movements. If she could have traced his steps, the pattern would form a perfect isosceles triangle. Under his breath, Duncan repeated, "Danger."

She took the warning to heart; his father said that he sensed things. And Alma had mentioned a curse on the town. "Danger means we should leave. Right now."

He ran away from her and disappeared behind a concrete wall.

She started after him. "Duncan, listen to me."

"Danger," came a louder shout.

The door at the top of the stairs slammed with a heavy thud. Fear shot through her. She spun around, staring toward the stairs. Though she saw no one, her sense of being stalked became palpable. That door hadn't blown shut by accident.

The lights blinked out. Darkness consumed her. Not the faintest glimmer penetrated this windowless tomb. Trapped. She thought of Teddy Fisher. Of the serial killer who liked women with long black hair.

Terror stole her breath. Where were the stairs? To her right? Her left? Her hands thrust forward, groping in empty space.

If she'd been here by herself, Madeline would have screamed for help. But Duncan was with her, and she didn't want to frighten him. "Duncan? Where are you?"

"Right here." He didn't sound scared. "Thirty-six steps from the stairs."

"Don't move." She listened hard, trying to discern if anyone else was here with them. The silence filled with dark portent. She moved forward with hesitant steps. Her shin bumped against a cardboard box. Her outstretched hands felt the cold that emanated from the walls. She pivoted and took another step. Was she going the wrong way? "Duncan, can you find the stairs?"

Instead of answering, he started counting backward from thirty-six. His strange habit came in handy; the boy seemed to know his exact location while she was utterly disoriented.

She bit back a sob. Even with her eyes accustomed to the dark, she couldn't see a thing.

"I'm at the stairs," Duncan announced.

She took a step toward his voice and stumbled. Falling forward to her hands and knees, she let out a yip.

"I'm okay," she said, though Duncan hadn't inquired. The only way she'd find the stairs was for him to keep talking. "Can you say the poem about starlight?"

Instead, he chanted, "She sells seashells…"

Crouched low, she inched toward the sound. When her hand connected with the stair rail, she latched on, desperately needing an anchor, something solid in the dark.

"Danger," he shouted.

Shivers chased up and down her spine. She had to get a grip, had to get them to safety. "I'm going up the stairs, Duncan. I'll open the door so we have enough light to see. Then I'll come back down for you."

"I can go. I'm very brave."

"Yes, you are." But she didn't want to take a chance on having him slip and fall on the stairs. "That's why you can stay right here. Very still."

As she stumbled up the steps in the pitch-dark, the staircase seemed ten miles long. By the time she reached the door, a clammy sweat coated her forehead. Her fingers closed around the round brass doorknob. It didn't move.

She jiggled and twisted. It was locked.

Panic flashed inside her head. A faint shimmer of daylight came around the edge of the door, and she clawed at the light as if she could pry this heavy door open.

Drawing back her fists, she hammered against the door. "Alma. Help. We're trapped in the basement. Help."

Behind her, she heard Duncan start up the stairs. She couldn't allow him to climb. In the darkness, balance was precarious, and Duncan wasn't like other kids. She couldn't hold his arm and keep him from falling, couldn't touch him at all.

"Wait," she said. "I'm coming back down."

Quickly, she descended. They'd just have to wait until they were found. Not much of a plan, but it was all she had. She sat beside Duncan on the second step from the bottom. "Here's what we're going to do. I'll count to five and you call for help. Then you count for me. Start now."

He yelled at the top of his lungs.

Then it was her turn. Screaming felt good. Her tension loosened. After she caught her breath, she said, "Now, we wait. Somebody will find us."

"My mama is already here," he said quietly. "She takes care of me. Whenever I get in trouble, my mama is close. She promised. She's always close."

His childlike faith touched her heart. "Your mama must be a very good woman. Can you tell me about her?"

"Soft and pretty. Even when she was crying, she smiled at me."

"She loved you," Madeline said. "And your daddy loves you, too."

"So do you," he said confidently. "From the first time you saw me."

In spite of her fear, Madeline breathed more easily. She should have been the one comforting him. Instead, this young boy lightened the weight of the terrible darkness with his surprising optimism. "You're very lovable."

"And brave."

"Let's yell again. Go."

At the end of his five seconds of shouting, the door at the top of the staircase opened. Daylight poured down with blinding, wonderful brilliance. Silhouetted in that light was the powerful masculine form of Blake Monroe.

"What the hell is going on?" he growled.

"Danger," Duncan yelled.

She heard Blake flick the light switch. "What's wrong with the lights?"

Duncan scrambled up the wooden staircase, and she followed. Stepping into the kitchen, she inhaled the light and warmth. This must be how it felt to escape from being buried alive. As she stepped away from the basement door, she wiped the clammy sweat from her forehead with the back of her hand. She and Duncan were free. No harm done.

When she saw the expression on Blake's face, her sense of relief vanished like seeds on the wind. The friendly camaraderie of this morning had been replaced by tight-lipped anger. "I want an explanation," he said.

She pushed her glasses up on her nose and cleared her throat. "Duncan and I decided to explore one room of the house before lunchtime."

"And you chose the basement." His hazel eyes flared. "There's all kinds of crap down there. Damn it, Madeline. What the hell were you thinking?"

She wouldn't blame this dreadful excursion on Duncan's insistence that they go to the basement. She was the person in charge. "We were fine until the door slammed shut. It was locked."

His brows arched in disbelief. He went down a step to test the doorknob, and the horrible darkness crawled up his leg. She was tempted, like Duncan, to warn him. To shout the word *danger* until her lungs burst.

Blake jiggled the knob. "It's sticking but not locked. You must have twisted it the wrong way."

She hadn't turned the knob wrong. That door had been locked. "Then the lights went out."

"There's a rational explanation. I have a crew of electricians working today."

She glanced toward Duncan, who stood silently, staring down at the toes of his sneakers. She didn't want to frighten the boy with her suspicions about Dr. Fisher or being stalked by the serial killer, but they hadn't been trapped by accident.

Blake yanked the door shut with a resounding slam and took a step toward her. Anger rolled off him in hot, turbulent waves.

Frankly, she couldn't blame him. It appeared that she'd made an irresponsible decision. When he spoke, his voice was low and ominous, like the rumble of an approaching freight train. And she was tied to the tracks. "You're supposed to be teaching my son. Not leading him into a potentially dangerous situation."

"All of life is potentially risky," she said in her defense. "Children need to explore and grow. New experiences are—"

"Stop." He held up a hand to halt her flow of words. "I don't need a lecture."

"Perhaps I'm not explaining well."

"You're fired, Madeline."

"What?" She took a step backward. Perhaps she deserved a reprimand, but not this.

He reached into his back pocket and pulled out a wallet. Peeling off a hundred-dollar bill, he slapped it down on the counter. "This should cover your expenses. Pack your things and get out."

Looking past his right shoulder, she saw Alma enter

through the back door with a couple of grocery bags in her arms. The housekeeper wouldn't be happy about Madeline being fired. Nor would Duncan.

But Blake was the boss. And his attitude showed no willingness to negotiate.

Though she would have liked to refuse his money, pride was not an option. She was too broke. With a weak sigh, she reached for the bill.

"Daddy, no." Duncan rushed across the kitchen and wrapped his skinny arms around his father's waist. "I like Madeline. I want her to stay."

Blake's eyes widened in surprise, and she knew that her own expression mirrored his. They were both stunned by this minor miracle. Duncan was touching his father, clinging to him.

As Blake stroked his son's shoulders with an amazing tenderness, she wondered how long it had been since Duncan had allowed him to come close.

The boy looked up at him. "Please, Daddy."

Blake squatted down to his son's level. Though Duncan's eyes were bright blue and his hair was a lighter shade of blond, the physical resemblance between father and son resonated.

Blake asked, "Do you want Madeline to stay?"

The hint of a smile touched Duncan's mouth. He reached toward his father's face with his gloved hand and patted Blake's cheek. "I like her."

With the slow, careful, deliberate motions used to approach a feral creature, Blake enclosed his son in a yearning embrace. A moment ago, he'd been all arrogance and hostility. Now, he exuded pure love.

Empathy brought Madeline close to tears. Her hand

covered her mouth. Staying at Beacon Manor was like riding an emotional roller coaster. In the basement, she'd been terrified. Facing Blake's rage, she was defensive and intimidated. As she watched the tenderness between father and son, her heart swelled.

The front doorbell rang.

"Get the door," Blake said to her.

Hadn't she just been fired? "I don't—"

"You're not fired. You're still Duncan's teacher. Now, answer the door."

Not much of an apology, but she'd take it. She needed this job. Straightening her shoulders, she walked down the corridor to the front door.

Standing at the entryway were two women. A cheerful smile fitted naturally on the attractive face of a slender lady in a stylish ivory suit with gray-blue piping that matched the color of her eyes. Her short, tawny hair whisked neatly in the breeze. Confidently, she introduced herself. "I'm Beatrice Wells, the mayor's wife."

Madeline opened the door wider to invite them inside. "I'm Madeline Douglas. Duncan's teacher."

When she held out her hand, she noticed the smears of dirt from crawling around in the basement and quickly pulled her hand back. "I should wait to shake your hand until I've had a chance to wash up."

"It's not a problem, dear." Beatrice gave her hand a squeeze, then turned toward her companion. "I'd like you to meet Helen Fisher."

As in Teddy Fisher? Madeline couldn't imagine that creep had a wife. "Are you related to Dr. Fisher?"

The frowning, angular woman gave a disgusted snort. "Teddy is my brother."

She stalked through the open door in her practical oxblood loafers. Her nostrils pinched and the frown deepened as she set a battered briefcase on the floor. She folded her arms below her chest, causing a wrinkle in her midcalf dress and brown cardigan. Though the month was July and the weather was sunny, Helen Fisher reminded Madeline of the drab days at the end of autumn. Everything about her said "old maid." Madeline suppressed a shudder. For the past couple of years, she'd feared that "old maid" would be her own destiny. If she stayed at this job long enough to put some money aside, she really ought to invest in something pretty and sexy. A red dress.

Beatrice Wells twinkled as if to counterbalance her companion's grumpy attitude. "Helen is our town librarian, and we're here to talk with Blake about the renovations."

"Beacon Manor is a historic landmark," Helen said. "The designs have to be approved by the historical committee."

"I really don't know anything about the house. My job is Duncan." She looked toward Beatrice. "I wondered if there was a baseball team in town. Something I could take Duncan to watch."

"We have an excellent parks and recreation program. There's even a T-ball program for the children."

Though Madeline wasn't sure if Duncan could handle a team sport, T-ball might be worth a try. "I'll certainly look into it."

When Blake came down the corridor toward them, he seemed like a different man. An easy grin lightened his features. He looked five years younger...and incredibly handsome. Even Helen was not immune to his masculine charms. She perked up when he warmly shook her hand. A girlish giggle twisted through her dour lips.

Given half a chance, Blake Monroe could charm the fish from the sea.

Chapter Five

As Blake escorted Beatrice Wells and Helen Fisher into the formal dining room with the ornate ceiling mural, he listened with half an ear to their commentary about the historical significance of Beacon Manor. In their eyes, the painting of cherubs and harvest vegetables rivaled the Sistine Chapel.

His thoughts were elsewhere. When he'd held Duncan in his arms, his blood had stirred. His son had smiled, actually smiled, and responded to a direct question. For the first time in years, Blake had seen a spark in his son's eyes.

Then Duncan had turned away from him and marched to his seat at the kitchen table for his usual silent lunch.

For today, one hug was enough. Maybe tomorrow…

Helen placed her fat leather briefcase on the dropcloth covering the carved cherrywood table and pulled out a stack of photographs. "These pictures were taken in the 1940s during an earlier restoration. Perhaps they'll be useful in recreating the ceiling mural."

"I've already ordered the paint," Blake said, "including the gold leaf. There's an artist in New York who specializes in historical restorations."

"Sounds expensive," Helen said archly. "I don't suppose my brother has set any sort of prudent financial limits."

Blake had submitted a detailed budget. Not that the expenditure was any of Helen's business. "You'll have to talk to Teddy about that."

As they moved to another room, he heard Madeline talking to Alma in the kitchen. How had she made such a difference with Duncan in such a short time? She lacked the expertise of the autism specialists he'd consulted. She wasn't a psychologist or a behaviorist. Just a schoolteacher.

For some unknown reason, his son connected with her. Was it her appearance? At first glance, he hadn't noticed anything remarkable about her, except for those incredibly long legs. When she took her glasses off, her aquamarine eyes glowed like the mysterious depths below the ocean waves. Was she magical? Hell, no. Madeline was down-to-earth. Definitely not an enchantress. And yet there was something about her that even he had to admit was intriguing.

He climbed the sweeping front staircase behind the two ladies from town. At the landing, Beatrice paused to catch her breath and said, "Duncan's teacher mentioned that you might be interested in signing your son up for one of the T-ball teams."

"Did she?" A baseball team? What was she thinking?

"Raven's Cliff might not have all the cultural advantages of a big city, but there's nowhere like a small town for raising children."

If Duncan did well here, Blake was ready to move in a heartbeat. "How's the real estate market?"

"Quite good." Beatrice warmed to him. "In fact, my husband and I are considering selling a lovely three-bedroom on the waterfront. Should I have Perry talk to you about it?"

"Sure."

He imagined himself living in this Maine backwater, planting a vegetable garden while Duncan played in the yard behind a white picket fence. Maybe his son could find friends his own age. Maybe a dog. Blake imagined a two-story slate-blue house with white shutters. The back door would open, and Madeline would step through, carrying a plate of cookies. Yeah, sure. Then they could all travel in their time machine back to the 1950s when life seemed pure and simple.

After he showed the ladies the one bedroom that had been repainted and refurbished with velvet drapes, they went back down the staircase to the first floor. Without being rude, he guided them toward the exit.

Standing at the doorway, Beatrice said, "Be sure to tell that nice young woman, Madeline, that the person to contact about the T-ball team is Grant Bridges. He's an assistant District Attorney. A fine young man."

He noticed a tremor in her voice. "Are you feeling all right, Beatrice?"

"Grant was almost my son-in-law," she said softly. "It's difficult to think of him without remembering my beautiful daughter. Camille."

He'd heard this tragic story before. It was part of the curse of Raven's Cliff. "I'm sorry for your loss."

They stepped onto the porch below the Palladian window just as Teddy Fisher's forest-green SUV screeched to a halt at the entrance. Blake remembered what Madeline had said about Fisher carrying a handgun and stepped protectively in front of the women.

Teddy sprang from the driver's-side door like a Jack-in-the-box with a goatee. With a fastidious twitch, he straightened the lapels of his tweed jacket. Every time Blake had dealt with Teddy, he'd been well-mannered, but he seemed distracted, unhinged. His small face twisted with strong emotion that might be anger. Or it might be fear.

Helen shoved past Blake and confronted her brother with fists on her skinny hips. "Well, well. If it isn't the mad scientist."

"We haven't spoken in months, Helen. At least try to be civil."

"Don't bother holding out an olive branch to me," she snapped. "You don't deserve my forgiveness."

"Your forgiveness?" His eyebrows arched. "I don't recall apologizing to you."

When he lifted his chin, Blake noticed that Teddy's shirt collar was loose. He'd been losing weight, had been under stress. Blake had heard stories about how Teddy's latest "scientific breakthrough"—a nutrient for fish—had caused a recent epidemic in Raven's Cliff.

"Bastard!" Oddly, Helen's facial expression mirrored that of her brother. "You ought to be in jail."

"At least I'm trying to do something with my life, working to enhance the Fisher name, like our grandfather."

"Grandfather won the Nobel Prize for science." Her voice rang with pride. "You're the booby prize."

"And I suppose it's better to play it safe like you? The town librarian? A manless crone who grows older and more dried up every day?"

"How dare you." She turned toward Beatrice, who watched with horrified eyes. "Your husband never should have allowed Teddy to buy the Manor."

Beatrice shifted uncomfortably. "There wasn't much choice, Helen. The abandoned property belonged to the town. After the hurricane, Raven's Cliff needed the revenue from the sale."

Frankly, Blake was glad that the Manor had only one owner. If he'd been forced to get approval from some kind of township committee, the restoration of the Manor and lighthouse would have been impossible.

Helen went on the attack again. "Damn you, Teddy. You hoarded your share of the family inheritance."

"And you frittered yours away."

"I invested in you," she said with hoarse loathing.

He gave a smug little grin. "Someday you'll get your investment back. I'm on the verge of a discovery."

She poked at him with a long finger. "The only way I'll ever be paid back is when you're dead."

Blake stepped in before this brother-and-sister reunion erupted into a physical fight. He grasped Teddy's arm and guided him away from Helen with a brisk, "Please excuse us, ladies."

Teddy walked a few paces before he shook Blake's hand off. "I'm sorry you had to witness that outburst. My sister has always been hot-tempered."

Blake glanced over his shoulder at the plain, thin woman whose angular face had gone white with rage. "Yeah, she's a real spitfire."

"She never believed in me. Not really."

"Was there something you wanted to talk to me about, Teddy?"

"I saw Beatrice and Helen arrive, and I just wanted to remind you that you're working for me. Not some idiotic historical society."

"I'm clear on who's paying the tab," Blake said.

"Well, good."

In his architectural redesign business, Blake came into contact with a number of eccentrics. He had to draw clear boundaries and didn't like the idea that Teddy had been watching the manor. "You know, Teddy, anytime you want to see the progress on the restoration, I'll try to accommodate you."

"Of course." The little man pulled a white handkerchief from his jacket pocket and dabbed nervously at his forehead. His beady little eyes darted. "It's my house, after all."

"However," Blake said, "while my family is in residence, you need an appointment to set foot inside. Otherwise, you're trespassing. And I don't deal kindly with trespassers."

"Is that a threat?"

"A friendly warning," Blake said.

Beacon Manor was only a job. Duncan's safety took precedence.

THAT NIGHT, after Duncan had gone to bed, Madeline finished unpacking in her bedroom. She'd found a place for all her clothing, set up her laptop and placed a few precious knickknacks around the room. There wasn't space for her books, so she'd left three full boxes in the back of her station wagon. All her other belongings had either been sold or given to charity, which was no great loss. Her apartment had been mostly furnished with hand-me-downs and inexpensive necessities.

At least, that was what she told herself. She ought to be glad to get rid of that worthless clutter, but her foster-home upbringing made her into a bit of a security junkie. She tended to hoard things for no other reason than to have them. That had to change. She needed to embrace the fact that she was unencumbered, free to pick up and leave at a moment's notice…the next time Blake fired her.

That man was an enigma. At times, he seemed to be the archetype of a dark, brooding genius who was passionate about his work. But he was also a loving father who clearly adored his son. When he was around Duncan, his barriers dropped, and she saw genuine warmth. Otherwise, he was arrogant, demanding. Sophisticated, but not much of a conversationalist.

Earlier this afternoon, he'd pulled her aside to offer a rational explanation for what had happened when she and Duncan were trapped in the basement. The door at the top of the staircase must have blown shut in a gust of wind. He pointed out that several windows had been left open to let in the warm July weather. One of the electricians working on the renovations had tripped the breaker switch, causing the lights to go out. Blake had insisted that the basement door wasn't locked.

She wanted to believe him, to accept the possibility that being trapped in the basement was nothing more than an unfortunate accident. Yet, she had sensed the danger that Duncan identified in shouts, and she fully intended to shove her potted ficus in front of the bedroom door before she fell asleep.

When she heard a tap on her bedroom door, she pulled it open. Blake stood there. He was dressed for the outdoors in a denim jacket and jeans. No matter what else she thought of him, Madeline couldn't deny the obvious. He was intensely handsome.

However, seeing him at her door, she assumed the worst. "Is something wrong? Does Duncan need something?"

"He fell asleep as soon as his head hit the pillow." A tender smile lit his features. "He let me kiss his forehead and tuck him in."

She couldn't take credit for his son's change of habit. The workings of Duncan's mind were a mystery to her. "He truly cares about you."

"It occurred to me," he said, "that it's a pleasant night. Would you like to take a walk on the grounds?"

"In the dark?"

"It might be better to do this while Duncan is asleep. There are several places I'd prefer he didn't explore."

His rationale made sense; she ought to be aware of the boundaries. "Let me grab a jacket."

She pulled a lightweight blue sweatshirt over her cotton blouse and khaki slacks. Since she was already wearing sneakers, she was appropriately dressed for a trek. Stepping into the hallway, she said, "Lead the way."

Outside, in the moonlight, she appreciated the pristine isolation and beauty of their surroundings. In last night's storm, the rugged forests had loomed and threatened. Tonight, the tall pines formed a protective boundary at the western edge of the property. A sea-scented breeze whispered through the high branches as they stretched toward the canopy of stars.

With his hands clasped behind his back, Blake walked along the road leading toward the lighthouse ruins. Moonlight cast mysterious shadows on the charred, tumbled-down tower.

"How was the lighthouse destroyed?" she asked.

"A fire and a freak category-five hurricane. It was about five years ago. That storm also did a lot of damage to the Manor that was never properly repaired."

"I can understand why someone would want to restore the Manor. It's a beautiful house. But why bother with the lighthouse? With GPS satellite navigational systems, nobody needs these old lighthouses anymore."

"Both the Manor and lighthouse are part of the legacy of the town. If you're interested, Helen Fisher dropped off a booklet about the history of Raven's Cliff."

"And the curse?"

"A legend that started when the town was founded. It's good for tourists. Everybody loves a ghost story."

"I suppose so."

"By the way, the lighthouse is off-limits to Duncan. Especially after the scaffolding goes up and reconstruction gets under way."

Obviously, a construction site was no place for a child. Nor was a basement. She never should have allowed Duncan to go down there. The echo of his voice rang in her mind. *Danger. Danger. Danger.* "What about the serial killer? The Seaside Strangler. Is he part of the curse?"

"He's real. Abducts young women, dresses them in white gowns, like brides, and drapes them in seaweed before he kills them."

A shiver ripped down her spine. The first time Duncan had seen her, he'd identified her with one of the victims. "That doesn't seem like a story that would draw visitors."

"Which is why the locals play it down. Tourism is the second most important industry in Raven's Cliff. Mostly, this is a fishing village."

He directed her toward the rocky edge of the cliff. Across the bay, the lights of the town glimmered. Fishing boats and other sailing crafts bobbed in the harbor. She saw the spire of a church and a few other tall buildings but nothing that resembled a skyscraper. Though she'd expected to find average dwellings and stores in Raven's Cliff, this picturesque view could have come from another century. "When was Raven's Cliff founded?"

"Late 1700s." He glanced down at her. "You're going to keep asking questions until I tell you the whole story, aren't you?"

She couldn't tell if he was irritated or amused. "I'll read Helen Fisher's booklet later. Just give me the short version."

"Captain Earl Raven owned the land. When he brought his wife and two small children over from England, his boat was shipwrecked on those rocks." He pointed toward a treacherous shoal. Even in this pleasant July night, the dark waves crashed and plumed against the rugged outcropping. "His wife and children were washed away and their bodies never found."

"Sounds like the town started with a curse."

"Could be. Captain Raven was involved in some shady dealings," he said. "Stricken with grief, he settled here and commissioned the building of the lighthouse with a powerful beacon. One night a year, on the anniversary of his family's death, he focused the beam on those rocks. His apprentice claimed that on that dark and scary night he saw Raven take a sailboat out to the rocks where he was joined by the ghosts of his family."

Pushing her glasses up on her nose, she peered down at the rugged coastline. Relentless waves crashed against the dark, jagged rocks. "A family of ghosts. What happened next?"

"After Raven passed away, the apprentice inherited the Manor. The town prospered and grew."

He went silent, and she turned toward him. His expression was utterly unreadable. She wondered if he was thinking of his personal ghost—his wife who had passed away only a few years ago.

"The townsfolk kept up the old traditions," he said. "Even after the lighthouse was no longer in use, the lighthouse keeper fired up the beacon every year on the anniversary. Until five years ago."

"The start of the curse."

He nodded. "The beacon wasn't lit at the appointed time. Somebody screwed up. Then came the fire that claimed the lives of the elderly lighthouse keeper and his grandson, Nicholas Sterling. The hurricane not only damaged the manor but destroyed a lot of other property in the town. Since then, Raven's Cliff has been plagued by bad luck."

"More than the serial killer?"

"Deaths at sea. Fishermen losing their boats. Strange disappearances. Recently there was a weird genetic mutation in the fish that caused an epidemic. And a couple of months ago, the daughter of the mayor was swept off the edge of the cliff in a gale-force wind. It happened on her wedding day."

"The daughter of Beatrice Wells?" Madeline remembered the determinedly perky smile of the mayor's wife. Beatrice didn't look like someone who had lost her daughter so recently. Either she was amazingly resilient or firmly in denial.

"There are rumors that the daughter, Camille, is still alive." He raised a skeptical eyebrow. "That ought to be enough story-telling to satisfy your curiosity."

"Perhaps."

When he started walking at the edge of the cliff, she chose the inward side to walk beside him. Though not afraid of heights, she was thinking about the bride who was whisked over the edge by a gust of wind. "These local legends are interesting. I could make the history of Raven's Cliff into a lesson for Duncan."

"I'd rather you didn't. I don't want him worrying about the curse. He's already picked up something he must have heard about Sofia Lagios."

"Which indicates an interest," she said. "Something I could use to focus his reading and writing skills."

"No serial killers," he repeated firmly. "Duncan has already had enough tragedy in his life."

She pressed her lips together to keep from arguing, but she didn't agree. Blake couldn't pretend that the death of Duncan's mother had never happened, especially since the boy talked to her ghost every day.

Chapter Six

Following the moonlit path at the edge of the cliff, Blake led her to the weathered, wooden staircase that descended forty feet to the rugged private beach. He hadn't decided how he felt about Duncan being allowed to explore in this hazard-filled area. Swimming was, of course, out of the question in these frigid northern Atlantic waters. Not to mention these treacherous currents.

He paused at the top of the staircase and watched as Madeline tentatively stepped onto the landing and peeked over the railing. Tendrils of her black hair had escaped the tight ponytail on top of her head and formed delicate curls against her pale cheeks.

The real reason he'd wanted to take this walk with her was to express his gratitude for whatever she'd done to cause Duncan to open up. Her work impressed him, but he didn't want to give the impression that she had free rein with her lesson plans. Left to her own devices, she'd probably be teaching his six-year-old son how to spell *homicide* and *strangulation*.

He needed to get a handle on this tall, slender school-teacher who had made such a huge impression on his son.

Who was Madeline Douglas? Her reticent nature made her almost invisible. She seemed organized, almost fastidious. And yet—by her own admission—she'd shown up on his doorstep without a penny to her name.

It shouldn't be so hard for him to figure her out. She was only an employee—another in the seemingly endless parade of tutors, teachers and nannies. But he knew she was different. Duncan cared about her; that made her special.

As she leaned out over the railing, he noticed the flare of her hips and the rounded curve of her bottom. She sure as hell didn't dress to show off her shape. Not in those prim little cotton blouses and baggy sweatshirts. Right now, the only skin visible was that on her trim ankles above her sneakers. His gaze swept the length of her legs. Too easily, he could imagine those legs entwined with his.

When she faced him, her eyes widened behind her glasses. "Where do the stairs lead?"

"To a private beach and several caves." He stepped in front of her. "I'll go first. If you slip, I can catch you. Hang on tight to the railing."

The wood-plank staircase, firmly anchored to the wall of the cliff, zigzagged like a fire escape. At the bottom was a cove of jagged rock that surrounded less than a mile of dark, wet sand. Moonlight shone on the churning waves, and the roar of the surf echoed against rock walls. Even on a temperate night like this, the rugged beach was lashed by wind and sea. The power of these untamed elements aroused his artistic nature, reminding him of life's fragility. The buildings he designed and restored—even skyscrapers and cathedrals—were frail shells compared to the timeless ocean.

She walked across the sand, leaving footprints, until she

stood at the edge of the foaming surf. "The water looks cold."

"And the undertow is deadly."

"I wonder," she said, "if there's any way I could bring Duncan down here. It's so beautiful."

"The problem with introducing Duncan to this area is that he might try to come here alone. Sometimes, he sticks to the rules. And other times…"

"He's headstrong," she said.

Her plain-spoken description amused him. His son's autistic behavior had been studied by teams of specialists who stated their theories in polysyllabic profusion: *Pervasive developmental disorder. Hypersensitivity. Asperger's Syndrome.*

She called it headstrong. If only life were so simple.

"For now," Blake said, "let's keep this area off-limits to Duncan."

"For now."

As she nodded, he studied the sharp outline of her jaw. Her features were too angular to be pretty, but her face had character. An interesting face. Appealing.

When she met his gaze, she seemed startled to find him watching her. Quickly, she looked down. Shyness? Or was she hiding something?

"Madeline, there's something I need to tell you."

"You're not going to fire me again, are you?"

"Hell, no. Why would you think that?"

"Because I've only been at the Manor for twenty-four hours, and you've already ordered me to get out twice."

Damn it, she made him sound like a total bastard. He pushed away his irritation. "I wanted to thank you. It's been months since Duncan has allowed me to hold him in my arms, to kiss his forehead, to tuck him under the covers. Thank you for this precious gift."

She darted a glance in his direction. "You're welcome."

"I want to build on this foundation. Tell me how you got my son to open up?"

She shrugged. "I haven't been following any special program. Mostly, I just treat him like a regular kid."

Not what he wanted to hear. In the back of his mind, Blake had been hoping for a teaching technique—a set of rules he could follow.

He strode across the sand. "This way to the caves."

"Of course," Madeline said, though she wasn't sure she wanted to go spelunking in the dark.

Carefully picking her way across the narrow strip of dark sand toward the wild shrubs near the cliff wall, she followed his lead. His expression of gratitude surprised her. Though he'd been visibly moved when he held Duncan in his arms, she never thought he'd attribute his son's openness to her.

At the inward side of the cove, craggy granite formations sloped down to the sea, like the arms of a giant reaching for the surf. Blake stepped onto the ledge and held out his hand to assist her. When her fingers linked with his, a powerful surge raced up her arm. His intensity frightened her while his strength drew her closer.

He helped her onto the ledge and steadied her by holding her other arm. Their position was almost an embrace. She met his gaze and saw starlight reflected in his hazel eyes. On this rocky promontory jutting into the sea, Blake was in his element, braced firmly against the wind and salt spray from crashing waves.

For a moment, she wished his touch meant something

more intimate. She wished for his affection, wished that this dynamic, talented man could care for her.

Releasing her arm, he pointed upward. "There's a shallow cave there. We'll have to climb."

"I see the opening." She had no desire to test her balance on these slippery rocks. "But let's not go there."

"I thought you were curious, ready for an adventure."

"Not if it means breaking my leg when I slip and fall." If she hadn't been firmly anchored to his hand, she might have stumbled right here. "Let me get my bearings. Where are we in terms of the lighthouse and the manor?"

He looked skyward as if he could discern their location by the position of the stars. "Do you see the trees up there? We're almost directly across from the entrance to the manor."

She hadn't realized that the cliff's edge was so close to the forest. No wonder he insisted on having Duncan accompanied on his outdoor excursions.

"The largest cavern is back on the beach."

"No climbing?"

"Not a bit."

"Let's check it out."

He helped her down from the ledge and crossed the sand to a gaping maw the size of a double-wide garage. A few standing rocks, taller than her head, shielded the entrance from view. "I can't believe I didn't see this giant hole before."

"It's the shape of the rocks and the shadows," he said. "Even in daylight, you might not notice the cave."

As soon as she stepped inside, the cold stone walls shielded her from the wind. An impermeable curtain of darkness hung before her. They had entered a place of eerie secrets. A dragon's lair.

"It's huge." Her voice dropped to a whisper. "Did smugglers and pirates once use these caves?"

"You'll have to read Helen Fisher's history of the town to learn the local superstitions."

Though she didn't consider herself psychic, she felt a deep foreboding. Bad things had happened in this cave—murders and intrigues by seafaring renegades. Or perhaps something had happened not too long ago. The curse of Raven's Cliff.

After a few steps into the darkness, she scooted back into the moonlight. Her memory of being trapped in the windowless basement was still too fresh. She had no desire to go deeper. "This is enough for me."

"Scared of the ghosts?" he teased.

"Not all ghosts are frightening, you know." Though she hated to risk making him angry, she felt it was important for him to know about Duncan's connection to his deceased mother. "Duncan has spoken to me about his mother."

"Kathleen."

When he whispered her name, a pall of sadness slipped over him. In the moonlight, she saw a haunted expression in his eyes. "Can you tell me about her?"

He raked his fingers through his dark blond hair. A nervous habit. "She was beautiful. Blond hair. Laughing eyes. She loved to dance. And she was a gourmet chef."

The combination of wistful sorrow in his voice and the strange atmosphere of the cave was almost too heavy for her to bear. Still, she wanted to know more. "Why did you and your wife choose to name your son Duncan?"

"Family name. I used to tease Kathleen that she'd named our boy after the cake mix."

"A major insult for someone who cooked from scratch."

"I guess so." He shook his head as if to clear the cobwebs on these buried memories. "When she didn't like one of my architectural designs, she called me Frank Lloyd Wrong."

"She had a good sense of humor."

"Kathleen was good at everything."

It was obvious that he still treasured her memory, still loved her. She doubted anyone would ever measure up to his deceased wife. "Before she passed away, was she aware of Duncan's disability?"

"She was spared that pain. Duncan was only three, almost four, when she died. He was always a goofy kid. A trickster. Loved to play games." His eyebrows lifted. "I never thought of this before. It was Kathleen who started his habit of counting his steps. When they came out the door of our brownstone, they counted the stairs. Up and down. Up and down the stairs."

Madeline wondered if the boy heard the echo of his mother's voice when he measured his steps. "She sounds like a good mother."

"A lot better at parenting than I was." He winced as if in physical pain. "I was building my career. Spent a lot of time away from home on different restoration projects. Always thought there'd be more time with Kathleen. Then, the cancer. I didn't know our days were limited."

Acting on an instinct to comfort him, she placed her hand on his arm. His muscles tensed, hard as granite. "You couldn't predict the future, Blake."

"After she died, I was even more of a workaholic. Couldn't stand being in the house where we'd been so happy. I sold it. We moved. I took every project that came my way. I was running day and night, running away from my sorrow, so caught up in my own pain that I lost track of Duncan. I was a damn selfish fool. I should have been there for Duncan. Should have…"

His voice trailed off in the wind.

There was nothing she could say to heal his grief and soothe his regrets. Her concern was his son. For his sake, she had to speak. "When Duncan and I were trapped in the basement, he told me that I didn't need to be afraid because his mother was watching over us. She's always there for him. He talks to her. She's a very real presence in his life."

"Like a ghost?" he asked angrily.

"An angel."

Anguish deepened the lines in his face. For a moment, she thought he might erupt. By poking into the past, she might have overstepped the bounds of propriety. He had a right to his privacy, his personal hell.

"An angel," he whispered. "I like that."

His tension seemed to ebb as he strode across the windswept sands. At the foot of the weathered wooden staircase, he turned toward her.

Nervously, she met his gaze, preparing herself for the worst. The man was so mercurial that she didn't know what to expect. He was capable of ferocious anger. And even greater love, like the abiding love for his wife.

The merest hint of a smile played at the corner of his mouth. "I'm glad you told me."

"Oh." She exhaled in a whoosh. "Not fired?"

His smile spread. When he rested his hand on her shoulder, she felt the warmth of connection. A warmth that sent her heart soaring. What would it be like to experience the force of his passion? To be swept away?

"You'll always have a place with me, Madeline."

This was where she belonged. With him. And Duncan.

Chapter Seven

After a few days with no major disasters, Madeline began to believe that she really was part of this odd little family. Duncan's carefully charted daily routine gave a rhythm to each day in spite of the arrival of roofers and bricklayers who were repairing the chimneys. The workmen kept Blake busy; she'd hardly been alone with him since their walk on the beach.

He'd been friendly—at least, what passed for friendly with this brooding architectural genius—and she couldn't complain about the way he treated her. Still, Madeline had hopes for something more. A real friendship, perhaps. Who was she kidding? Her fantasies about Blake skipped down a far more sensual path—one that was totally inappropriate.

While Duncan ate his solitary lunch, counting each chew before he swallowed, she delivered a lunch tray to Blake's studio on the first floor. Originally, this room had been a formal library, and one wall was still floor-to-ceiling books. The antiques that would one day occupy this space had been removed for expert refinishing, and Blake used a purely functional, L-shaped desk and black metal file cabinets. His computer, phones and fax machine rested amid stacks of papers, invoices and research materials.

His back was toward her as he stared at blueprints taped onto a slanted drafting table near the west-facing window. Without turning, he said, "Just leave the lunch on the table. Thanks, Alma."

"It's me," she said quietly, not wanting to disturb his concentration but wanting him to notice her.

He pivoted. His unguarded gaze sent a bolt of heat in her direction. "Hello, Madeline."

Those two simple words unleashed an earthquake of awareness through her body. She placed the lunch tray on his desk before she dropped it. He'd shaved today. The sharp line of his jaw was softened by a dimple at the left corner of his mouth.

Pushing her glasses up on her nose, she broached the topic she'd wanted to discuss. "I was wondering if I could possibly get an advance on my paycheck. There were a few things I wanted to purchase. For Duncan."

"I'd be happy to pay for anything my son needs."

"These aren't teaching supplies." His prior teachers had compiled an excellent selection of books, educational materials and computer programs. "It's other stuff."

He came around the desk. "What kind of stuff?"

She hated asking for money, even though she had a good reason. Avoiding his direct gaze, she mumbled, "Baseball equipment. Duncan and I have been playing catch in the afternoon and I—"

"Catch? You and Duncan?"

"After his regular lessons are finished," she assured him. "We've gotten to the point where we can throw the ball back and forth five times without either of us dropping it."

"Five catches? That's better than Duncan has ever done before. Why didn't you tell me?"

"You've been so busy with the work crews arriving."

"I'm never too busy for my son. I made that mistake once already, and I won't make it again. Duncan is my number-one concern. The whole reason I took this job in Raven's Cliff was so I could spend more time with him in a relaxed, stress-free atmosphere."

She couldn't imagine a situation involving Blake that would be without stress. The air surrounding him crackled with electricity. "Of course, you're welcome to join us."

He sat on the edge of his desk with his arms folded across his broad chest. "I've tried physical activities with Duncan before. It's never turned out well."

"Playing with me is no challenge because—as Duncan is delighted to point out—I'm just a girl. There's more pressure with you."

"Why?"

She shrugged. "He doesn't want to disappoint you. He can play catch, but he's no Roger Clemens or Wade Boggs."

"Clemens and Boggs. Legendary Red Sox players."

"I'm from Boston."

"Uh-huh." He nodded slowly. "It's high time for me to get involved in this baseball teaching plan of yours. Can't have you raising my boy to be a Sox fan. This family roots for the Cubs."

She drew the obvious conclusion. "You're from Chicago."

"Born and bred in the 'burbs. One sister, one brother and a German shepherd named Rex." He went behind his desk, opened a drawer and pulled out a checkbook. "No problem with an advance, Madeline. You've made excellent progress with Duncan. He's still letting me hug him and touch him."

The boy hadn't yet extended that invitation to her. Nor had his father, she thought ruefully.

Blake handed the check to her. Reading the amount, her eyes popped. Five hundred dollars. "This is too much."

"And I'll be paying for his sports equipment out of my own pocket. Getting my son his own glove, his own bat. Damn. That's every father's dream. Give me an hour to make sure everything here is running smoothly. Then we'll all go into town. You and me and Duncan."

"We'll be ready." A trip into Raven's Cliff sounded like an adventure. She hadn't left the Manor since she'd arrived and was beginning to feel cloistered.

She returned to the kitchen just as Duncan set down his spoon. Without a word, he hopped down from his chair and marched toward the family room. His schedule called for quiet time, which usually meant he sat at his computer.

Since Alma was nowhere in sight, Madeline cleaned up the dishes and loaded them in the dishwasher. For the past couple of days, she'd been using this after-lunch lull as her own personal time to read or fiddle around on her laptop. Today, she was too excited to sit still.

She climbed the staircase to her bedroom and tucked Blake's check into her wallet. With this money, she'd open a bank account and start rebuilding the chaos of her life. As if to underline her thoughts of reconstruction, she heard hammering from the roofers overhead. Progress, she thought. Progress in many directions.

With a bounce in her step, she returned to the family room where Duncan sat on the floor amid a clutter of toy trucks. Instead of following her regular pattern of relentlessly tidying up the mess, she pushed aside a couple of books on the large sectional sofa, grabbed the remote from the top of the television and sat facing the screen.

Duncan cast a curious glance in her direction. He seldom asked what she was doing. Planning ahead wasn't part of his behavior, and she was careful not to make that sort of demand. Instead, she announced, "I'm going to watch a baseball game on TV. You're welcome to join me."

She tuned in to a Boston station on cable. The game hadn't yet started, and a local news program was on. The smoothly coiffed anchorman glanced down at his notes, and she caught the words *diamond heist* and *estimated loss of over seven hundred thousand dollars*. Quite a haul. She couldn't even imagine what seven hundred thousand dollars' worth of diamonds looked like.

A mug shot of her brother appeared on the screen. "A suspect is in custody."

Oh my God, Marty. What have you done?

The anchorman's words hit her like a hail of bullets. "The jewels have not been recovered. Police are looking for an accomplice."

Her thumb hit the off button and the TV went blank.

"Where's the game?" Duncan looked up at her. "I want to watch the baseball."

"In a minute."

Her gut clenched. The ache spread through her body. She wanted to bury her face in her hands and sob, but she didn't want Duncan to be alarmed. Or, even worse, to start asking questions. *Damn it.* She'd known that Marty was up to no good.

A few months ago, he'd shown up on her doorstep. Miserable and broke, he'd told her that he wanted to go straight but owed a lot of money. He had to pay it back or he'd be hurt, maybe even killed. How could she turn him away? He was her brother.

Fearing the worst, she'd emptied her bank account and savings to give him the cash he needed. Instead of thanks, he ran her credit card up to the max. She had no way to pay rent or any of her other bills.

Maybe she could have worked things out, but Marty got into a knock-down, drag-out argument with her landlord. She had to move. There was always the option of going home to live with the Douglases, but she'd been too humiliated. They'd always told her she couldn't trust Marty. Even as a child, he'd been a liar and a thief. But pulling off a diamond heist?

Damn you, Marty. Two weeks ago when she'd confronted him, he put on a cool, smug attitude and told her not to worry because he was coming into a lot of money. From a debt that was owed to him. Hah! She should have suspected the worst. But she'd purposely closed her eyes, wanting to believe that maybe, just maybe, her brother was telling the truth.

When she got the call from Alma about the teaching position with Duncan, it had seemed like a godsend. At least Madeline would have employment and a place to live. Being far away from Marty in Maine seemed prudent.

The night before she left, he'd showed up at her apartment. Instead of his usual smooth talk, he'd been agitated and sweaty. Had he just stolen those diamonds? He'd collapsed on the floor in her empty apartment and slept like a log. The next morning, he was gone but had left a note that said: "The police might come around asking about me. Don't tell them anything."

That should have been her cue to go directly to the police. But she didn't have anything to tell them. She didn't know what her brother had done. Until now.

Looking up, she saw Duncan standing only a few feet away from her, watching her curiously, almost as though he could read all the dark thoughts swirling inside her head.

Were the Boston police looking for her? The TV anchorman had mentioned an accomplice. Would the authorities think she'd aided and abetted in the jewel heist? Would she end up in jail for no other reason than her brother was a criminal?

No, she wouldn't allow Marty to destroy her life any more than he had already.

No, she wouldn't talk to the police. She had no useful information for an investigator.

No, no, no. This wasn't happening.

If she kept her mouth shut, she'd be safe. *Don't make trouble. Stay in the background.* As a child in foster care, she'd learned those lessons well.

Forcing a smile, she looked at Duncan. "The baseball game should be on now."

He climbed onto the sofa, and she turned on the television. A wide-angle shot of Fenway Park appeared on the screen.

Duncan pointed and said, "Ninety feet from base to base. It's a square."

"But they call it a diamond," she said, cringing at the word. Over seventy thousand dollars' worth of diamonds.

When the national anthem was played, she stood on shaky legs. "Every game starts with that song about our country. We stand and place our hand over our heart to show respect."

Duncan pointed to the flag on the screen. "Fifty stars for fifty states."

She looked down at his smooth blond hair as he stood at attention. The innocence of this troubled boy soothed her own fears. If she concentrated solely on Duncan, she might be able to forget her own problems.

As the Red Sox took the field, she ran through all the numbers that would appeal to him. First base, second and third. Nine players on a team. Distance from the pitcher's mound to home plate was sixty and a half feet.

"When we play catch," he asked, "how far apart are we?"

"I don't know. We'll have to measure."

"Good."

Duncan leaned forward. He seemed to be completely caught up in the game. As they counted balls and strikes together, her fears lessened. The symmetry of the game comforted her. All of life was about balance. Ups and downs. She and her brother had always been at opposite ends of the spectrum.

Suddenly, Duncan jumped off the sofa. He ran close to the television, then back to the sofa. He was breathing fast, almost hyperventilating.

"You want to show me something," she guessed. "Something on the television. What is it?"

At that moment, Blake sauntered into the room.

Duncan's skinny arm pumped back and forth like a metronome at the television screen. "Gloves," he said.

"That's right," his father said. "Baseball players in the field need to wear a glove to catch the ball."

"Not them." Duncan shook his head. "The man with the bat. The batter. He has gloves."

And so he did. The man at the plate wore leather gloves on both hands. Madeline hadn't even thought of this advantage. When Duncan played baseball with other kids, he could wear gloves and not be considered strange at all.

"Batting gloves," Blake said with a wide smile. "Do you want to get some batting gloves?"

"Yes." Duncan's blue eyes actually seemed to sparkle. "I want to be a baseball player when I grow up."

Wearing gloves was a simple solution, allowing him to be around other children without touching. She wished that her own problems could be so easily solved.

Chapter Eight

The central business district in Raven's Cliff clung desperately to its heritage as a historic New England village. Tourists enjoyed the ambience. Blake didn't.

As a general rule, he disdained any shop with "Ye Olde" in the name. Still, he preferred shopping in the village to visiting a superstore with drab neutral walls and overstuffed rows of undifferentiated merchandise. He appreciated that most of these businesses—even those that were self-consciously cutesy—were mom-and-pop operations that had been in the family for years.

He parked on the street opposite the Cliffside Inn, a three-story bed-and-breakfast with genuinely interesting features, including a two-story tower with cornice and a cone-shaped roof.

"Charming," Madeline said as she peered through the windshield at the house. "Look at the roses. Those gardens are brilliant."

"I stayed at the Inn on my first visit to Raven's Cliff," he said. "The interior has nicely maintained Victorian antiques and some very good art, but the real draw is the proprietor, Hazel Baker. She's a character."

When he stepped out of the SUV and held the back door open for Duncan, he spotted Hazel in the front yard with a garden hose. Her long, rainbow-colored skirt caught the July breeze and swirled around her sturdy legs as she waved vigorously and called out, "Good afternoon, Blake. Lovely weather, eh?"

"Nice to see you, Hazel."

He liked that they knew each other's name. This sort of small-town atmosphere was exactly what he wanted for Duncan. In a place where people looked out for each other, a kid like Duncan had a shot at being accepted.

Though he would have liked to cross the street and introduce Madeline to kooky Hazel, who declared herself to be Wiccan, Duncan was tugging on his arm. "Hurry, Daddy. We have to get my gloves."

"Sure thing, buddy."

He linked his hand with his son's. Though he knew from experience that Duncan could, at any moment, pitch a tantrum or go stiff as a board, he savored this moment. Having a kid who was excited about baseball was so damn normal. Once again, he had Madeline to thank for this phenomenon.

As she strolled along the wide sidewalk on the other side of Duncan, she smiled at every person they met—tourists and residents alike. Straightforward and direct, this woman had nothing to hide. Behind her glasses, her gaze scanned constantly, taking in all the details of the neatly painted storefronts and the various eateries, most of which were off-limits to Duncan because of his dietary restrictions. No sugar. No wheat. No salt.

Madeline was quick to point out a sign in the bakery window. "Gluten-free, sugar-free muffins."

"This is where Alma picks up our bread."

"Maybe later, we could get a treat."

Duncan yanked his hand. "First, my gloves."

They crossed the street to enter the general store—a large, high-ceilinged space with an array of tourist products up front. A tall, barrel-chested man with curly red hair and a beard to match approached them. "Hey, now. Aren't you that architect fella working up at the Manor?"

"That's me." Blake shook his hand. "I'm Blake Monroe. This is my son, Duncan. And his teacher, Madeline Douglas."

"I'm Stuart Chapman. What can I do you for?"

"Sporting equipment," Blake said.

When Stuart reached up to scratch his head, Blake noticed the tattoos on his forearms. Inside a heart with bluebirds on each side was the name *Dorothy*. "I don't have a whole lot of stock, but I can order anything you need."

"It's for Duncan," Madeline explained. "He'd like to start playing T-ball."

"You're in luck," Stuart boomed as he lumbered toward the rear of the store. "We've got a T-ball league for the youngsters, and I carry all the equipment. Hats, balls, gloves."

"Gloves," Duncan said loudly.

Blake knew that tone of voice. A signal of tension building inside his son. A warning.

Hoping to avoid an outburst, Blake went directly to the batting gloves and selected one that ought to fit his son. Opening the package, he held it out. "Try this."

As soon as Duncan slipped the leather-backed glove onto his right hand, he beamed. Finally, this was a glove he could wear without being teased.

"The other hand," he said.

"Well, now," Stuart said. "Most batters just use the one. No need for two."

"Not really," Madeline said. "All the major leaguers wear gloves on both hands."

"Eh, yup. You're right about that." Stuart chuckled. "Duncan could be the next Wade Boggs."

"Boggs," Blake muttered. "Another Red Sox fan."

They picked out another glove, which Duncan insisted on wearing, then selected mitts for each of them, bats and a tee for practicing. All things considered, this was one of the most blissfully normal shopping trips he'd ever had with his son.

He eyed the bases. "I'm thinking we might go all the way and set up our own practice field at the Manor."

Stuart chuckled again. "I'd like to see the look on Helen Fisher's face if you do."

"True," Madeline said. "I doubt they ever had a baseball field at the Manor."

Stuart shrugged his heavy shoulders. "That Helen. She's a stickler for historical accuracy."

The hell with Helen Fisher and the good folks of Raven's Cliff Historical Preservation Committee. This was his son. "We'll take the bases. And a couple of duffel bags to carry everything."

"Good for you." Stuart clapped Blake on the shoulder. "When my four boys were young, I'd have chosen them over historical accuracy any day of the week. Building the athletes of tomorrow. Ain't that right, Duncan?"

"Yes."

Before Blake could stop him, Stuart reached down and ruffled the hair on Duncan's head. Then he turned away to gather up their equipment.

Duncan's reaction to physical contact with a stranger was immediate. His lips pressed together in a tight, white line. His eyes went blank. He seemed to stop breathing.

Dreading the worst, Blake squatted down to his son's eye level. "Are you okay, buddy?"

Madeline was also leaning down. She whispered, "Tell your daddy what you saw."

Duncan's chest jerked as he inhaled. "That man is very sad. Dorothy is sick. His wife. Must be brave. Must hope for the best."

"Thank you for telling us," Madeline said.

Duncan's eyes flickered to his father's face. His breathing returned to a more normal rhythm. He licked his lips, blinked, then he held up both hands. "Gloves."

Blake studied his son's face. The signs of tension had already faded. He ran to the front of the store where Stuart was ringing up their total expenditure on an old-fashioned cash register.

Crisis averted.

Madeline stepped up beside him. "Do you think Duncan really saw something? That he sensed what Stuart was feeling?"

"No," he said curtly. Dealing with an autistic child was difficult enough. He damn well refused to start worrying about his son being a psychic weirdo. Leave that nonsense to the kooks like Hazel at the Cliffside Inn.

While Stuart was tallying up their haul, Blake thought he recognized the mayor walking past the front window. "Is that Perry Wells?"

"Yup." Stuart frowned. "I'm surprised he's got the nerve to show his face."

"Why?" Madeline asked.

"There's been letters in the newspaper about corruption in the mayor's office." He ran the back of his fingers across his beard. "Anonymous letters."

"A cowardly way to make accusations," Madeline said. "How can you believe someone who won't sign their—"

"Excuse me," Blake said. He handed his wallet to Madeline. "Pay for this. I'll be right back."

His reason for talking to Mayor Perry Wells had nothing to do with accusations or political corruption. A few days ago, when the mayor's wife had come to the Manor, she'd mentioned the possibility of a house for sale. A beachfront three-bedroom. It was worth taking a look.

On the sidewalk, he called out, "Mayor Wells."

The tall man in a khaki-colored suit came to an abrupt halt and darted a nervous glance over his shoulder as if expecting someone to throw a pie in his face.

Blake strode toward him. "Good afternoon, sir. I'm not sure if you remember me. Blake Monroe."

"Of course. Call me Perry." His practiced politician's smile lifted the corners of his mouth.

When he shook Blake's hand, his fingers trembled. Those anonymous letters must be having an effect, which made Blake wonder about the validity of the charges. "I'm enjoying my time in Raven's Cliff."

"And you're doing important work at the Manor. Vital to our town."

"Nice to be appreciated," Blake said, "but I'm just doing my job. Teddy Fisher is paying me very well."

At the mention of Teddy's name, the mayor's elegant features tensed, but he was quick to recover his poise and launch into what sounded like a prepared speech. "When the restoration of the Manor and the lighthouse are complete, when the beacon shines forth across the sea, it will signal a new era of prosperity for Raven's Cliff. A full recovery from our tragedies. A lifting of the curse."

Blake couldn't let that remark pass. "Surely a man such as yourself doesn't believe in a curse."

"It's symbolic. On that dark day when the lighthouse was destroyed, the hearts and minds of the citizens in Raven's Cliff were poisoned."

"You must be pleased that Teddy has taken on the responsibility of restoring the lighthouse."

"Why do you keep mentioning him? Teddy isn't…" He paused, visibly shaken. What had Teddy Fisher done to this man to provoke such a response?

Blake dropped the topic, which was really none of his concern. "A few days ago, your wife visited the Manor and mentioned a house you might have for sale."

"Are you thinking of settling in our town?"

"Considering it."

Perry reached into his tailored jacket and took out a polished gold case. He handed his card to Blake. "Call my office, and we'll make an appointment. I'd be happy to have you as one of my constituents."

Pocketing the card, Blake returned to the general store to gather up their purchases. Two duffel bags full.

After they'd dragged the baseball equipment back to the car, he was ready to head back to the Manor. So far, this had been a pleasant outing. He didn't want to push their luck.

When he unlocked his driver's-side door, Madeline objected. "Wait. I had a few things I wanted to do. A stop at the bank. And I noticed a dress in one of the store windows."

He glanced over at Duncan, who paced in a circle around a streetlamp. "What do you think, buddy? I say we hang around while Madeline goes shopping."

Duncan stopped in front of his father. With an expression typical of any other six-year-old, he rolled his eyes. "I guess."

"We can watch the fishing boats."

"Yes," he shouted.

"It's settled," Blake said. "We'll wait for you at the docks. On the bench outside the Coastal Fish Shop."

"Thanks, boys."

As she hurried down the street ahead of them, he was struck by the feline gracefulness of her walk. Most of the time, she looked like a drab little house cat, but when she moved with a purpose, her long legs stretched and strode like a more exotic creature. Maybe a cheetah.

He and Duncan took their time going back into town. They stopped in the bakery for a gluten-free, sugar-free cookie and a couple of bottled waters. Then they went to watch the boats.

Beyond the end of the commercial district, the street sloped down to the fishing docks. Not many tourists came to this fishy-smelling area where hardworking crews off-loaded the day's catch from boats that had been battered by years at sea. They were coarse men, scarred and weathered from their heavy, sometimes dangerous labor. Blake admired their grit and determination.

Drinking their bottled water, he and Duncan sat on a bench outside Coastal Fish—a business that had almost gone under during the recent epidemic that had been traced to genetically altered fish.

Across the cove, the ruins of the lighthouse seemed picturesque. He pointed it out to Duncan. "There's where we live."

"I don't see our house."

"It's behind the trees. But there's the lighthouse."

He stood and craned forward for a better view. "I'm not supposed to go to the lighthouse."

"You got that right."

He counted four steps forward, then four steps back, then forward again. His gaze stuck on a group of fishermen. Two grizzled older men smoked and laughed. The third was younger, more refined in his features. He turned toward Duncan and stared for a long moment.

"Four, three, two, one." Duncan was back at his side. He pressed his face against Blake's arm. Under his breath, he mumbled unintelligible words.

"I can't hear you," Blake said.

"She sells seashells," Duncan said. "Seashells by the seashore. Seashells."

He was tired. After a full afternoon, he needed to get back to the Manor. They needed to go. Now.

Fortunately, Madeline appeared on the docks with a bag from the dress shop hanging from her arm.

When Blake looked back toward the fishermen, the younger man had vanished.

Chapter Nine

After they returned to the Manor, Madeline left Blake and Duncan to sort out the new baseball equipment while she went up to her room. Kicking off her sneakers and socks, she stretched out on the duvet. A sea-scented breeze through the open window stirred the dangling teardrop crystals on the quaint little chandelier, causing bits of reflected light to dance against the walls like a swarm of fireflies.

She closed her eyes, thinking she might catch a nap, but there were too many other worries. At the bank in Raven's Cliff, she'd cashed the check from Blake but hadn't opened an account, fearing that her location might be traced by the Boston police. As if withholding her name from a bank account would hide her whereabouts. She had to file a change of address form to make sure her creditors knew her location. She couldn't just disappear. If the police wanted to find her, they would.

And she couldn't keep her brother's crime a secret, certainly not from Blake. Alma knew Marty. It was only a matter of time before Alma heard about the diamond heist and said something. It would be a hundred times better if Blake heard about Marty from her own lips.

She left the downy-soft bed and went to the window overlooking the grounds at the front of the house. It was after five o'clock; the roofers and other workmen had knocked off for the day. The scheduled dinnertime was in less than an hour. For now, Blake and Duncan were playing catch.

Her own games with Duncan had been casual, tossing the ball and reciting rhymes while pausing to pick wild-flowers. With his father in charge, catch took on the aspect of a male-bonding ritual. Not only did he throw the ball back and forth, but also straight up in the air and bouncing wildly across the grass. Blake chased after one of those grounders, scooped it up and rolled across the ground in a somersault and lay there. Duncan ran to him and pounced on his chest. Both were laughing.

So normal. So sweet.

Stepping away from the window, she took the red dress from the bag and prepared to hang it in her closet. The silky fabric glided through her fingers. Never in her life had she purchased anything so blatantly flirty.

She tore off her everyday outfit and slipped the dress over her head. The sleeveless bodice criss-crossed over her breasts and nipped in at the waist, giving her an hourglass shape. The skirt floated gracefully over her hips and ended at her knees. The clerk in the store had complimented the hem length, which would have been too long on a shorter woman.

The clerk had also given her another bit of information that she needed to share with Blake, even though he probably wouldn't want to hear it.

On tiptoe, she twirled in front of the antique mirror above the dressing table. A red dress. Definitely not the sort of outfit for an old-maid schoolteacher.

A bit of jewelry at the throat might be nice. She tried on various lockets and pearls. None of her accessories seemed chic enough for the dress. The same was true for her clunky, practical shoes.

She reached up on top of her head and unfastened the clip holding her hair in place. The heavy black curls tumbled around her neck and shoulders. Still watching herself in the mirror, she went to the bed and sat on the edge, crossing her legs. When she leaned forward, the plunging neckline showed a nice bit of cleavage.

Tonight she would tell Blake about Marty and the diamond heist. Why shouldn't she? Her brother might be a crook, but she had nothing to hide.

A tap on her bedroom door startled her, and she bolted to her feet. "Who is it?"

"Blake."

She snatched her other outfit from the bed where she'd discarded it. She ought to change clothes, slip back into her teacher persona. But why? If she ever intended to wear this red dress outside the confines of her own bedroom, she ought to get a second opinion from Blake.

Tossing her other clothes into the closet, she straightened her shoulders. "Come in."

The instant he saw her, his eyes lit up. "Wow."

His appreciative grin was worth every penny she'd paid for the dress. "I wanted to try it on," she said. "To see if it looked as good here as in the shop."

He came forward, took her hand and raised it to his lips for a light kiss that sent a tingle up her arm. He murmured, "You're beautiful."

"Thank you." She dropped a small curtsy and reclaimed her hand. Unaccustomed to such outright admiration from the opposite sex, she experienced a nervous flutter in her tummy. He wasn't lying. He really liked the dress.

"Turn around," he said.

She twirled on her bare toes, and the fabric floated away from her legs.

"I need shoes," she said. "I don't have a single pair that looks right with the dress."

"I like your bare feet," he said as he came closer.

She was about to complain about the size of her feet, something that made her nearly as self-conscious as her height, but the glow from his hazel eyes mesmerized her. She froze where she stood, watching with almost detached curiosity as he reached toward her.

His fingers glided through her hair as he removed her glasses. "The color of your eyes is striking. Aquamarine."

He stood close enough that she could see him clearly without her glasses. His lips parted.

She tilted her chin upward, waiting to accept whatever he offered. Gently, he kissed her forehead just above her eyes. She wanted so much more.

When his hand clasped her waist, she responded. Leaning toward him, the tips of her breasts grazed his broad chest. She reached up and caressed the firm line of his clean-shaven jaw.

Then he kissed her for real. His mouth pressed hard against hers. A fierce heat blazed in her chest, stealing her breath. She clung to him, caught up in this magical moment, lost in a red-dress fantasy. The most handsome man she'd ever seen was kissing her. Her? Tall, gawky Madeline? It didn't seem possible. Somehow, in a moment, she'd transformed into a swan.

His tongue slid across the surface of her teeth and

plunged into her mouth. She responded with a passion she'd never known existed within the boundaries of her humdrum life. She was spinning and dizzy, yet utterly aware of every incredible sensation.

When they separated, she was gasping. She wanted him close where she could see him. Wanted many more kisses. A thousand or so.

AFTER DINNER, Duncan knew he shouldn't be outside. But there was still a little bit of sun in the sky, and the stars weren't out. He wanted to set up the bases so he and Daddy could play real baseball.

He carried one of the flat, white rubber bases into the yard and dropped it. "Home plate," he said.

First base was ninety feet away. How many steps was that? He picked up another base from the duffel bag and turned toward the forest. He counted his steps all the way to fifty, then fifty again, then backward ten. This wasn't right. Too far.

Then he heard her voice, high and pretty, singing the seashell song.

"Temperance," he called out.

He dropped the base and ran toward the sound. He wanted to show her his new batting gloves and tell her about the trip to Raven's Cliff.

Where was she? He looked around the tree trunks but didn't see her white dress and long gold hair.

"Don't play hide-and-seek." He turned around in a circle, looking everywhere. "That's a baby game."

There were so many shadows in the forest. He heard the waves at the bottom of the cliff. He was never, ever supposed to go near the cliff alone. But he wasn't by himself. Temperance was here.

She stepped out from behind a tree trunk. "Hide-and-seek is not a baby game."

"I play baseball." He reached into his pocket and pulled out his new gloves. "This is what baseball players wear."

She turned up her nose. "Can girls play?"

"Mostly not. Madeline tries, but she's not as good as my daddy."

"I dislike baseball." Temperance stamped her foot. "How should I like a game I cannot play?"

"Don't be mad." He hid his gloves behind his back. "You're my friend, Temperance. I'll teach you how to play."

"Really?"

"I'm making a diamond." He remembered how she said she could never go into the Manor. "It's outdoors."

She wrinkled her brow. "There is danger in the Manor. In the basement."

Danger. The basement was dark and scary, but nobody had hurt him when he got trapped with Madeline. "I'm not afraid."

"Come with me." She laughed. "There is something I must show you."

He followed her through the trees to the very edge of the cliff. She was standing way too close. The wind blew her dress and her red cape. "Come back, Temperance."

She pointed along the ledge. "Do you see that man?"

He squinted through the gloom. The sun was gone. Night was coming. "I can't see him."

"Step out here by me."

This was wrong. His daddy would be very angry if he found out. Taking very careful baby steps, he left the shelter of the trees. The wind blew right in his face, but he didn't run away. He wasn't a scaredy-cat.

Far away along the cliffside, he saw the man. "Who is he?"

"The lighthouse keeper's grandson. Nicholas."

"Is he the bad man? The one who hurt Sofia?"

"Goodness, no." Her mouth made a pretty little bow. "He is very unhappy, as well he should be. He caused the fire in the lighthouse and brought the curse on Raven's Cliff."

Duncan didn't know much about curses. But starting a fire was bad. "I want to go back to the yard."

"Come play with me." She twirled on her tiptoes at the edge. "You are my best friend."

He had never been anybody's best friend. He wanted to please Temperance. He took one more step forward. The waves roared. The noise filled up his head and made him dizzy.

Temperance sang, "She sells seashells."

"By the seashore," he responded. "I want to go back."

"And so we shall." She darted into the forest.

Duncan turned to follow, but he couldn't move. His feet seemed to be stuck at the rocky edge of the cliff. He looked out at the waves and saw a boat coming. Danger. The boat could run into the rocks. Danger.

The wind pushed him closer to the edge.

Someone grabbed him. He couldn't see the person, but he felt skeleton fingers close tightly around his arm and shake him until his teeth rattled.

Black darkness rolled over him. Hate-filled darkness.

Chapter Ten

"Alma, have you seen Duncan?"

"Sorry, boss."

Blake left the kitchen and headed upstairs. He'd only left Duncan alone for a moment while he went into his studio to tidy up the details of the day's work. Now he couldn't find the boy. He checked the bedroom. The bathroom. Maybe he was with Madeline.

Blake paused outside her bedroom door. Only a few hours ago, a simple knock on this door had introduced him to a vision in red and the most incredible kisses. Her slender body had fitted so perfectly in his arms that she seemed to be made for him—created to fulfill his exact specifications. The subtle fragrance of her hair had enticed him. Her lips had been soft and sweet. He hadn't wanted to stop. His instincts told him to seize the moment, to make love to her—this amazing, feminine creature with the mesmerizing eyes, cascading black hair and long legs.

A thin leash of propriety had held him back. She was Duncan's teacher and doing a damn good job with his son. Blake would be a fool to jeopardize that relationship by taking Madeline to bed.

He tapped on the door.

She opened. Her glasses were perched on her nose. Her hair was twisted up on top of her head, and she wore loose-fitting jeans and a baggy T-shirt. In reverse metamorphosis, she'd gone from a butterfly to a plain caterpillar.

"What's wrong?" she asked.

"I can't find Duncan."

Twin frown lines furrowed her brow. "Do you think he went outside?"

"I sure as hell hope not. I've told him a hundred times that he's not to go outside after dark." Apparently, a hundred wasn't enough. "Damn it. Every time I start thinking that he's like other kids, he pulls something."

"Seems to me that a little boy wanting to play outside is the least strange thing in the world." She stepped into the hallway and closed the door behind her. "Let's go find him."

She made everything sound so simple. As they descended the staircase, he said, "You understand, don't you? Duncan isn't like other kids?"

"He's special." In the foyer, she turned to him. "When I was in town, buying my dress—"

"Your red dress." He couldn't help grinning as he thought of that silky fabric sliding over her body.

Behind her glasses, she gave him a wink. "I talked to the clerk about Dorothy. Do you remember Dorothy? She's the wife of Stuart, the man who owns the general store. When Stuart touched Duncan, he said Dorothy was sick."

Blake remembered. He'd seen the Dorothy tattoo on Stuart's beefy forearm. "And?"

"Dorothy is battling MS. Duncan sensed that from touching her husband."

He didn't like where this conversation was headed. "Let's not get started on the psychic crap."

"Duncan might be an empath. Someone who can sense the emotions of others with just a touch. Don't you see, Blake? That's good news."

He didn't see anything positive about having his son take on yet another abnormality. "Why good?"

"I'm not an expert," she said, "but empathy seems to be somewhat the opposite of autism. Instead of being trapped in his own little world, Duncan might be supersensitive to the moods and feelings of others."

"And that's good?"

"Difficult," she admitted. "Can you imagine what it must be like to know what other people are feeling?"

If anyone but Madeline had suggested this theory, he would have scoffed. But she'd been right before.

And his beloved Kathleen had been sensitive. Always talking about feelings, she seemed to know who he could trust and who he should avoid. Her first impressions were always on target. Autism was supposed to have a basis in genetics. What if the same were true for empathy? What if Duncan inherited that ability from his mother?

Blake's gaze dropped to the patterned tile floor in the foyer. Near the door were the duffel bags holding the baseball equipment. One was missing. Duncan must have taken it.

He was probably outside right now, setting up the baseball diamond. "Let's go find my son."

Outside, the dusk had settled into night. He strode across the unkempt grassy area until he saw the glow of moonlight on home plate. Duncan had been out here.

Madeline pointed to another base that was nearer the trees. His son was nowhere in sight.

"Duncan," he called out. "Duncan, where are you?"

Anxiously, he looked toward the lighthouse. The charred, jagged tower held a dark foreboding. For a young boy, danger was everywhere. Climbing around on that lighthouse presented formidable hazards. Not to mention the cliffs with their fierce winds and uncertain footing.

Even more than the natural perils, Blake feared the human danger. Until now, the Seaside Strangler had only attacked young women. But Duncan had known the name of Sofia Lagios. He might have witnessed something suspicious, might be a threat to this predator.

From the corner of his eye, Blake caught a flash of movement. Heart pounding, he raced toward the trees. "Duncan."

Madeline was close beside him. When he looked into her face, he saw a reflection of his own panic. They were near the cliffs. The wind howling through the branches sounded like a cry for help.

As he stepped closer to the edge, he looked down and saw the gloves on the ground. Duncan's batting gloves. Oh God, no. He knelt and picked up the limp little gloves.

How could this be happening? Blake couldn't lose Duncan. He couldn't. Not his son. Not his precious child.

Fear paralyzed him. His heart stopped.

He couldn't bring himself to look over the edge, couldn't bear the thought of seeing Duncan's small body crumpled on the rocks below, his blue eyes staring sightless into the dark.

"Back this way," Madeline said. She tugged on his arm. "Come on, Blake."

"What?"

"I heard something. A shout. Back toward the house."

Desperately hoping that she was right, he fought his way through the low-hanging branches until they were back at the yard.

He saw Duncan stumbling toward the house.

Frantic, Blake dashed toward him, gathered the child up in his arms and held on tightly. "Are you all right? Are you hurt?"

Duncan's small body trembled. Over and over, he mumbled, "Danger, danger, danger."

"It's okay," Blake assured him. Waves of relief rushed through him. His cheeks were wet with tears. "It's okay, Duncan. I've got you. You're safe."

He carried the boy back to the manor. Inside, in the light, he could examine his son for possible injuries. In the kitchen, he sat Duncan on the countertop.

Alma poked her head around the corner. "Heavens, what's going on?"

"Get the first-aid kit," Blake ordered. He stared into his son's pale face. There was a smear of mud on his cheek, but Blake didn't see blood, thank God. "Duncan, can you hear me?"

"Yes."

"Are you hurt?"

The boy grabbed his own arm below the shoulder. "He held on to me here. And he shook me. He hates everybody. They don't treat him right."

"Who did this to you?" Blake immediately thought of Dr. Fisher and how he was always lurking around the grounds. If that bastard had laid a hand on his son...

"What did he look like?"

Duncan's eyelids drooped. His shoulders sagged forward. "Danger. Don't go in the basement. Danger."

Alma placed the first-aid kit on the countertop beside Blake and stepped back. Madeline stood on the other side. Blake was only marginally aware of their presence. His entire focus was on his son. "Who shook you, Duncan?"

"I don't know." He leaned forward, almost toppling from the counter. "Bedtime."

"He's exhausted," Madeline said. "Maybe in the morning, he'll remember more."

Not likely. Duncan's attention span was short-lived. By tomorrow, he would have forgotten this entire incident. "Why were you near the cliff? I've told you again and again how dangerous that is. You're not ever to go—"

A sharp jab in his ribs stopped his tirade. Madeline glared at him. "Bedtime," she said.

Duncan had scared him half to death with this escapade, and the boy knew better. "He needs to hear this."

"He needs you."

Her steady gaze grounded him. Blake had every right to be angry, but more than that, he was thankful and relieved. Now wasn't the time for scolding. He kissed the boy on the top of his head. "I love you, Duncan. I'm so glad. So glad that you're safe."

"Nicholas," Duncan said. "I saw Nicholas."

"Is that who grabbed your arm?"

Duncan frowned. "Nicholas. The lighthouse keeper's grandson."

That wasn't the answer Blake wanted to hear. Nicholas Sterling the Third had died five years ago when the lighthouse was destroyed.

AFTER DUNCAN went to bed, Madeline joined Blake in the studio downstairs. They needed to discuss what had happened to his son. Someone had frightened Duncan. A predator. "In my opinion," she said, "we should report this Nicholas person to the police."

"I don't think so."

"Why not?"

"Nicholas Sterling is dead."

She sank into the chair opposite the desk. "But Duncan saw him. Was he a ghost?"

"Obviously not." Blake stood in front of his drafting table where several blueprints were taped. "The only way my son would know that name and the fact that Nicholas Sterling was the lighthouse keeper's grandson is if someone told him. That same person must have mentioned the name of Sofia Lagios."

She couldn't imagine anyone so depraved. Telling stories about curses and murder victims to an innocent child? "Who would do that? Why?"

Blake picked up a T-square and held it against the blueprint. "Could be Helen Fisher, who is obsessed with the history of Raven's Cliff. Could be her nutball brother."

"Teddy." She'd despised that nasty little man since she'd bumped his car. "Sometimes he wanders around on the grounds."

"It's his property."

"That certainly doesn't excuse him. Why would he grab Duncan and scare him?"

Blake stared intently at the blueprints. "Both times when Duncan got himself lost in the night, he was warned about danger in the basement. Whoever keeps frightening him doesn't want him to go down there."

When she and Duncan had disobeyed that warning, they'd been trapped. No matter how many times Blake gave her a logical explanation for what had happened, she knew better. Maybe someone had been trying to scare them. "You might be onto something."

He tapped his forefinger against the blueprints. "I've noticed anomalies in the structural measurements regarding the basement. We need to check it out."

Fear rippled around the edges of her consciousness. Go back into that overwhelming darkness? "Maybe we should call the police."

"And tell them what? My son saw a ghost who told him not to go into the basement?"

A little boy's nightmare vision wouldn't be taken seriously. "You're right."

"We should explore now. While Duncan's asleep." He lightly stroked her cheek. "If you want to stay here, it's okay. I'll understand."

Now was her chance to back down. She had nothing to prove, had never claimed to be courageous. But he needed her, and she liked the feeling of being able to help. "I want flashlights. Several flashlights."

The appreciative light from his hazel eyes warmed her heart. "Don't worry, Madeline. I won't let anyone—human or ghost—hurt you."

He crossed the studio to the closet near the door. From the top shelf, he took down a locked box which he placed on the desk while he flipped through a set of keys in the top drawer.

Unlocked, the box revealed an automatic handgun and a holster—lethal protection against any threat that might live in the basement. Knowing they would be armed should have made her feel safer. Instead, her blood ran cold.

Chapter Eleven

They left Alma in Duncan's room, keeping watch over him while he slept. Madeline had a cell phone to call the house-keeper in case of trouble. She stashed the cell in the left back pocket of her jeans. In the other back pocket was a small penlight. In her right hand was a heavy-duty metal flashlight—just in case the electricity malfunctioned again.

Together, she and Blake descended the wooden stair-case.

With the lights on, the musty concrete basement didn't appear too frightening, yet the word *danger* echoed inside her head. *Danger, danger, danger.* She looked for spiders on the dusty, broken shelving that leaned drunkenly against one wall. The creaks and groans of the old house made her think of ghosts walking across the floorboards above their head. Oh, she hoped not. There was enough to worry about without bringing in threats from the supernatural.

She followed Blake as he picked his way through the fat, heavy support beams and framed walls that divided the space into haphazard rooms.

Shaking off her sense of foreboding, she asked, "Why aren't there any windows down here?"

"This house was built in the late 1700s. A long time before finished basements." Blake adjusted the blueprints in his hand and turned to his left. "Originally, this was probably a pantry for preserves. Then a wine cellar. In later years, there was a coal chute for the furnace."

"Which means there must be another way out."

"There was." He pointed to the blueprint. "When the furnace and water heater were upgraded, the chute was plastered over."

Despite the lack of windows and doors, the musty air stirred as they walked through it. Motes of dust that hadn't been disturbed for years swirled near her feet. The cold seeped through her sweatshirt to her bones, and she shivered. "Doesn't seem safe to have only one way out."

"I'll need to add another exit if I do upgrades down here."

She followed Blake behind one of the walls. The current furnace and water heater were fairly modern, probably only ten or fifteen years old, housed in the cleanest part of the basement. Behind the next wall was a filthy pen of heavy wood.

"Coal bin," Blake said as he kept moving.

Stacked haphazardly in corners of the makeshift rooms were cardboard cartons, old furniture and discarded odds and ends. Paint cans. A rolled-up sheet of linoleum. Several sheets of paneling.

"Junk," Blake said. "Unfortunately, I can't trash this stuff until I sort through it. There could be something of value."

"Maybe that's why someone warned Duncan to stay away from the basement. A hidden treasure."

"Maybe."

He went around another wall, then pivoted and came back in the opposite direction. His intense concentration on the blueprints reminded her of Duncan's single-mindedness, but Blake wasn't the least bit boyish. Not with those muscular shoulders. Not with the holster fastened to his belt.

She tiptoed behind him. "Could there really be a treasure?"

"Beacon Manor is the real deal, full of valuable antiques. Anything could be stashed down here." At the far eastern end of the basement, he ran his hand along the concrete. "There could be a hidden room."

"Is that why you keep checking the blueprints?"

"There are several discrepancies in the measurements," he said. "Most notable is a difference of eighteen inches between the upstairs floor plan and the basement, which could be explained by poor draftsmanship."

"Or a secret room."

A rising excitement replaced her cold dread. They had embarked on a real-life treasure hunt. She imagined rare artworks, priceless antique silver, a pirate's chest full of gold doubloons.

He pulled a sheet of plywood away from the wall, revealing nothing but more concrete. A daunting pile of clutter stood between them and the last bit of wall. Moving all that junk would be filthy work.

"I have another idea," Blake said.

She followed him as he retraced his steps to the coal bin. Blake climbed over the heavy boards blackened by ancient soot. With some trepidation, she followed. "Now what?"

"When you said the coal bin provided another way out, it got me thinking. All the outer walls are concrete, except for here. This could be a door. A crude door that was built over two hundred years ago."

"I don't see it."

"Look hard." He felt along the rough-hewn boards at the rear wall. His hands were immediately covered with thick black grime. "Do you feel that, Madeline? A breeze."

She heard the anticipation in his voice, but she didn't feel the breeze, didn't see the door. "I don't—"

"Got it." His fingers closed around a ridge in the wood. "A hinge."

In a moment, he'd found the latch and opened the secret door. A whisper of chill air swept over her. Beyond the entrance was nothing but darkness.

She turned on her flashlight and shone the beam into the open space—an earthen tunnel that led straight down. "A secret passageway."

Beaming as though he'd unearthed the treasures of King Tut's tomb, he turned to her. "This is a first for me. I've worked on some really old properties. Ancient. Mysterious. A villa in Milan. A small castle in Tuscany. And I've never discovered a secret passageway before."

She didn't share his enthusiasm. A passageway leading out meant that other people could secretly enter the house, which might explain how some nefarious person could have been sneaking into her room. That person could be lurking down there right now, hidden in the darkness. "Where do you think it goes?"

"There's only one way to know for sure. Bring the flashlight closer."

Instead, she drew back. Her feet rooted to the filthy floor of the coal bin. "What if someone's down there?"

"Then we've found what we're looking for." He drew

his automatic pistol from the holster. "I can carry this if it makes you feel better."

It didn't. The idea of a shoot-out in a dark cave terrified her. "I don't think we should do this. We should come back tomorrow with plenty of lights. And a police escort."

"How many times in your life will you discover a secret passageway? Come on, Madeline. Take a chance."

She'd never been a risk-taker. Those few times in her life when she'd acted against her cautious instincts—like when she'd trusted her brother—had resulted in disaster. But Blake's eyes enticed her. His eagerness to explore would not be denied. "You go first."

"I'll need the flashlight."

Reluctantly, she handed it over while keeping the smaller one for herself. "I'll be right behind you."

He stepped into the darkness. Slowly, he walked through the tunnel that appeared to be carved from the stone. The earth floor slanted down at a steep angle; they descended through bedrock.

The beams of their flashlights barely cut into the thick darkness—so heavy that she felt as though she was suffocating. The sound of her own breathing echoed in her ears. She shivered as an icy draft brushed her cheeks. God, it was cold.

The only way she could keep going forward was to concentrate on Blake's back. She followed him as closely as a shadow.

"The floor seems to be leveling out," he said. "There's a curve ahead. An intersection with another tunnel."

What if this tunnel turned into another? And another. What if they'd entered a labyrinth? She wished Duncan were here to count their steps. They could be lost forever.

When Blake halted, she bumped into him. "What is it?"

"A cave."

Peeking around his shoulder, she watched the beam of his flashlight as it played across a high, craggy ceiling. Massive boulders clumped on the floor like the crude furniture of a giant. His flashlight beam reflected on a small, opaque puddle of water, reminding her that they were near the shore. "Do you think this cave reaches all the way to the beach?"

"Oh, yeah. The tunnel we came through was man-made. This is natural." He pointed his flashlight to the right. "This way. Watch your step. There are lots of loose rocks."

She stumbled along behind him, trying to guess the distance from the manor to the shore. Half a mile? It felt like more, seemed like they were walking forever. Climbing over piles of rock, slipping through odd-shaped spaces as the cave widened and narrowed.

"I can hear the ocean," Blake said.

She heard it, too. The crashing of waves outside the cave. The darkness thinned. The air freshened. Excited that they were almost out, she dodged around him. Then slipped. Then fell.

She landed hard on her backside.

Blake was immediately attentive. He took her hand and pulled her to her feet. "Are you okay?"

"More embarrassed than hurt." She reached into her back pocket and took out the smashed cell phone. "Which is more than I can say for the phone."

He played his flashlight over her hands, then lifted the beam to her face. "We're almost out."

And she was proud of herself for taking the risk. "This isn't like anything I've ever done before. I'm glad I'm here."

"So am I."

He pushed stray wisps of hair off her forehead and gently kissed her lips—a reminder of their passion when she was wearing the red dress.

As they moved forward again, his flashlight shone on a plain, rectangular structure about the size of a trailer. Was someone living down here?

They approached the door, found it unlocked and entered. A switch turned on overhead lights, illuminating an open space with tables lining the walls, two large refrigerators and a desk. The generator that powered the lights must have also activated a fan because she heard the hum of a ventilation system. Stacked near the door were several wooden crates and packing materials. Resting on the tables were microscopes and laboratory equipment.

She examined a large centrifuge and read the label on the side, "Fisher Laboratories."

"Son of a bitch." Blake rummaged through the desk. "Teddy Fisher moved his lab down here."

"No wonder he's always creeping around the Manor."

"Technically, this property belongs to him. The private beach is part of the estate."

"But why? Why would anybody put a laboratory here?" She wished that they had stumbled across a chest of pirate's gold. Nothing good would result from this discovery. "This is all wrong."

INSIDE THE makeshift lab, Blake slammed a desk drawer. He was tempted to rake his arm across the surface of the lab tables, sending beakers and instruments flying. What the hell was Teddy trying to pull? His motive had to be criminal. "The only reason to put a lab here is to keep it secret."

"You said something about Teddy's experiments and an epidemic."

"He was looking for a nutrient to make fish bigger and more prolific."

"Not a bad idea," she said. "Bigger fish. More fish. That sounds like an economic boon for the town."

"Teddy's plan was a hell of a lot bigger than Raven's Cliff." The first time Blake had met the little scientist, Teddy had been bubbling with excitement, patting himself on the back so vigorously that he could have dislocated a shoulder. "The fish experiment was supposed to be his claim to fame. A cure for world hunger."

"But it backfired."

"In a big way." He tried to remember details of the stories he'd heard secondhand. "The fish weren't hurt. But people who ate them fell ill. Some died."

"That's murder," she said. "Why is Teddy walking around free? Why isn't he in jail?"

He'd wondered the same thing. "I looked into the situation. I had to."

"Of course you did. You wouldn't want to be hired by a murderer."

Actually, Blake's ethical concerns were secondary. Most of the wealthy, powerful people he'd worked for weren't Boy Scouts. If he started turning down projects because his clients weren't entirely innocent, he'd soon be left with nothing better to do than charity work for churches.

His main reason for wanting to know about the charges against Teddy was monetary; he didn't want to move to Raven's Cliff if the guy paying the bills was going to prison. "Teddy wasn't charged."

"Why not?"

"The curse."

The corner of her delectable mouth pulled into a frown, and he could tell that she didn't like what she was hearing. Primly, she said, "Please continue."

"A lot of the townspeople and the fishermen themselves blamed the epidemic on the curse. The gods of the sea are angry, and the spirit of Captain Raven is offended." A load of superstitious crap. "The only way to lift the curse is to rebuild the lighthouse and shine the beacon."

"Which made them anxious to have you get started."

He'd been welcomed with open arms. "I was assured that Teddy was in the clear. He voluntarily closed down his laboratory operation."

"Apparently not." She took the damaged cell phone from her pocket and punched the keys. "It's definitely broken."

"What are you doing?"

"We need to inform the proper authorities about Teddy's secret lab. He was clearly up to no good."

If he had ever felt the need for a moral compass, he need look no further. Madeline had the earnest eyes and determined chin of a crusader—a defender of underdogs, losers and endangered species. He usually found those traits to be tedious and incompatible with his creativity. Rules were made to be broken.

After Kathleen died, he'd preferred women who were free and easy, who left before breakfast, who wanted nothing but a one-night stand. Madeline was the opposite; she'd always expect him to do the right thing. "I'll bet you never break the rules."

"I try not to," she said.

"You use the turn signal even when there aren't other cars behind you."

"Yes," she said.

"If a clerk gives you change for a twenty when you gave them a ten, you return the extra."

"And I tip twenty percent, even if the waitress is surly. I don't cheat on my taxes. Don't jaywalk. I follow the recipes exactly when I cook."

"No risks. No adventures."

"I like order." She took a step toward him. Her voice softened to a whisper that made those solid values resonate with a purely sensual undertone. "I'm not a risk-taker. Sorry if that disappoints you."

His arm slipped around her slender waist and pulled her snug against him. "Who says I'm disappointed?"

"Most men are."

He nuzzled her ear and felt her body respond with a quiver. At this moment, he wanted to give her all the stability her heart desired. "I'm not most men."

She kissed him with a passion that seemed at odds with her need for order. Messy and wild. He didn't try to make sense of it. Just leaned into the kiss and enjoyed.

Breaking away from him, she said, "We should get back to the Manor."

To his bed. Making love to her was becoming more and more inevitable. Damn, he was ready.

As they stepped out of Teddy's secret lab, they were blinded by the darkness of the cave. Taking charge, Blake aimed the beam of his flashlight toward the secret passage, then in the opposite direction. "Let's keep heading toward the shore."

"Agreed. I don't want to go back through that passage unless I have to."

He led the way, circling an outcropping of stone that

kept the location of the lab hidden. Through another chamber, then into the final cave where the stone walls were damp with salt spray and the bright moonlight beckoned them toward the roaring surf.

"Wait," she said. Her flashlight pointed at the rocks near the edge of the cave, and she picked up a necklace made of shells. "Duncan has a shell like this."

Before he could respond, he heard a moan. A weak cry for help. Just outside the cave, something was moving. Blake handed his flashlight to Madeline and drew his handgun. "Stay back."

On the rocks outside the cave, Blake saw him. Teddy Fisher. Or what was left of him.

Struggling for every inch, Teddy crawled—dragging himself across the rocks. One of his legs was bent at an unnatural angle. His head was bloody. His eyes swollen shut. His dapper gray suit was torn and smeared with blood.

He'd been beaten by someone who knew how to make it hurt.

Chapter Twelve

Instinct drove Madeline forward. No matter how much she disliked Teddy Fisher, the man was seriously injured and needed help.

Blake caught hold of her arm. "No closer," he warned. "He might be armed."

She shone her flashlight back toward the cave. The person who had beaten Teddy might still be nearby. Might have been following them. Might be biding his time before he lashed out at them. What if there was more than one attacker? What if they were facing an army?

Blake handed her the gun. The heft of it surprised her. She'd never held a firearm before, hated when the kids in her classes pretended to shoot each other. Guns weren't toys.

Blake knelt on the rocks beside the injured man, rolled him onto his back and frisked his clothing.

Teddy's face was grotesque. Inside the neat circle of his goatee, his lips were bruised and bloody. Dark crimson blood streaked across his forehead. Each breath he drew caused him to wince.

He was trying to speak.

"What is it?" Blake asked. "Teddy, who did this?"

The swollen lips moved, but the only sound he made was a guttural moan. He convulsed. His body went limp.

Blake tore open Teddy's shirt.

"What are you doing?" she asked.

"Looking for other wounds. Shine the flashlight down here." He pushed aside the blood-stained white shirt. Using his fingers, he gently probed the harsh, red welts that crisscrossed Teddy's rib cage. "The blood seems to be coming from his head and other abrasions. He wasn't stabbed or shot."

But beaten to within an inch of his life. She turned away, couldn't stand to look. What kind of person could possibly inflict so much damage on another? To what purpose?

Blake stood. "There's got to be internal bleeding. He needs a doctor. Madeline, do you know CPR?"

In a couple of teacher-training sessions, she'd taken lessons. But she had never practiced life-saving techniques on another human being. "Not well enough."

"One of us needs to stay with Teddy. The other has to go to the house and call an ambulance."

Both alternatives sounded equally terrible. Facing unknown dangers on the way to the house? Staying here with the crashing waves and dark cave, watching over a dying man? She didn't know how she could manage to do either. Never in her life had she been heroic.

Blake stood and peeled off his jacket. "We need to move fast. He's fighting for his life."

"You're right." She swallowed hard. "Of course, you're right."

"Stay or go?"

Though she might encounter danger on the way to the

house, she'd be better at running than staying here to help Teddy. If he died under her watch, she couldn't live with that guilt. "I'll go."

"Take the gun," Blake said. "If anyone comes near you, shoot. Don't worry about aiming. The noise should keep them back."

"Okay."

"If I hear a gunshot, I'll come running." He squeezed her shoulder. "You can do this."

Though she didn't share his confidence, she turned on her heel and ran. In one hand, she clutched the flashlight. The other held the gun. Neither comforted her.

Scrambling across the uneven rocks on the shore, she moved faster than she would have thought possible. In minutes, she had reached the staircase. Moonlight shimmered on each stair, but she only saw shadows—formless shapes, threatening outlines.

Her heart pounded against her rib cage. In spite of the night breeze, sweat beaded across her forehead. As she climbed, the muscles in her legs throbbed, more from tension than exertion. Common sense held her back, warned her to be careful. But she had to get to the house, to summon the police. They needed the help of the authorities, and Teddy desperately needed a doctor.

At the top of the staircase, she drew huge gulps of air into her aching lungs. The beam of her flashlight slashed across the tree trunks of the forest that separated her from the Manor. Fierce gusts of wind chased over the edge of the cliff.

Before her fears took solid form, she plunged into the trees and fought her way through, shoving tree branches out of her way, stumbling, falling and rising again. She emerged on the other side. Across the yard, she could see the house. Only one light shone from the windows. The light from her own bedroom.

That could not be. She'd left the light off.

Though she couldn't see clearly from this distance, a shadow passed behind her bedroom curtains. Was it him? The person who attacked Teddy Fisher? He could be in her bedroom. Only a few steps away from Duncan.

The fear she felt for herself was nothing compared to her need to protect the child. She ran full out with her legs churning and arms pumping. She would not, could not allow anyone to hurt Duncan.

At the front door, she stabbed her key into the lock. Barely pausing, she charged up the staircase and down the hall. Into Duncan's room. In the faint glow of a night-light, she saw him sleeping. His lips parted as he breathed steadily, peacefully. A sweet, innocent boy. Protected by his mother, an angel.

Madeline turned back toward the corridor. She leveled the gun. If anyone came near Duncan, she'd have no trouble pulling the trigger.

The hall light went on, and she blinked. Standing near the bathroom was Alma. In her hand, she held a gun. "What's going on?" she demanded.

"Why do you have a gun?"

"Why do you?"

Her chin thrust out. Though Alma's face without her usual makeup showed her age, Madeline caught a hint of a younger woman. A woman she'd known many years ago. Her foster mother. Always yelling, thriving on conflict. Alma hadn't been mean, but angry. So very angry.

She shook away the memory; Madeline wasn't a helpless child. "What were you doing in my room?"

"I heard a noise." Alma looked down at the gun and seemed almost surprised that she was holding it. Immediately, she lowered the muzzle. "Sorry, honey. I was a little scared."

As well she should be. The vicious attack on Teddy Fisher gave validity to all of Madeline's vague fears. It was time to call the police.

As SOON AS the ambulance and paramedics arrived, Blake raced back to the house where he was greeted by Alma. Though a fresh coat of makeup smeared across her face, she couldn't disguise the tension at the corners of her eyes.

"Is he dead?" she asked.

"Hanging on by a thread." Teddy had never regained consciousness. Every ragged breath he inhaled seemed like his last. The external injuries were horrific, but Blake suspected worse damage had been done to his insides. Ruptured organs. Internal bleeding. "Where's Duncan? Where's Madeline?"

"Family room," Alma said. "Should I make coffee?"

"I'd say so. In a couple of minutes, we'll have a house full of cops."

He ran upstairs to wash the blood from his hands and change into a clean shirt. No need to scare Duncan by looking as though he'd been through a war. The circumstances would be traumatic enough for his overly sensitive son.

The police would have questions for the boy, namely who had grabbed him earlier tonight? If Duncan started talking about the ghost of Nicholas Sterling, things could get complicated.

In the family room, he found Madeline reading a book of rhymes to Duncan, who was still wearing his flannel pajamas. Her voice was low and soothing. Though her hair was a mass of tangles, she managed to appear calm.

Not the way she'd been when they'd found Teddy outside the cave. Then she'd been terror-stricken. Her delicate face had turned as white as ivory. Every muscle in her body had trembled, and she'd looked as if she was on the verge of fainting. It had taken a lot of courage for her to make it back to the house and call 911.

Duncan looked up, saw Blake and vaulted off the sofa. He ran to his father, who hoisted him into his arms and held him close.

"It's going to be okay, buddy." Blake stroked his son's fine blond hair. "Everything is going to be okay."

"What happened, Daddy? Madeline said you'd tell me."

"A man was badly hurt." The fewer details, the better. "Pretty soon, the police are going to come here and ask us some questions."

Duncan pulled back so he could look into his father's face. "Real policemen?"

"That's right."

The boy considered for a moment, digesting this information. Then he shrugged. "Okay."

"When we talk to the real policemen, we have to tell the truth. Isn't that right, Madeline?"

"You bet." The color had returned to her cheeks. The smudges of soot on her chin and forehead would have been cute if the expression in her aquamarine eyes hadn't been so solemn and serious.

His own feelings were more akin to euphoria. They'd been in a dire situation and had escaped intact. He'd been lucky as hell that whoever attacked Teddy hadn't stayed around to finish the job.

Apparently, Madeline took the wider view. A man had been brutally beaten. There was a dangerous person on the loose. Primly, she said, "Before the police arrive, I should change clothes."

Still holding his son, he held out his other arm toward her, pulled her close and gave her a hug. "You did good," he said.

"The night isn't over yet."

As she left the family room, he carried Duncan into the kitchen where he smelled the aroma of fresh brewed coffee. Alma had also laid out mugs, plates and napkins. She slid a tray of frozen baked goods into the oven.

Blake made a mental note. If he wanted Alma to perform in the kitchen, all he needed to do was to promise a houseful of handsome young cops.

The short end of the rectangular kitchen table fitted up against the wall, and Blake seated Duncan in the chair nearest the wall where he'd be protected from accidental touches from the police. After providing his son with bottled water to drink and a coloring book to keep him occupied, he left Alma watching Duncan as he went to answer the doorbell.

Two uniformed cops arrived first. The taller officer had red hair like the proprietor of the general store, and the metal name tag pinned above his front pocket said Chapman.

Blake shook hands. "Is Stuart Chapman your father?"

"That's right. All four of us Chapman boys are on the force." His proud grin and the sprinkle of freckles across his nose made him look more like a choirboy than an officer of the law. His eyes widened as he scanned the entryway. "I haven't been inside Beacon Manor since I was a kid singing Christmas carols."

"Most of the rooms are under construction. You'll need to watch your step."

"I'll do that, sir." He cleared his throat and tried to look official. "Can you tell me how many people are currently living at the house?"

"Myself, the housekeeper, my six-year-old son and his teacher." Blake glanced down the hallway toward the kitchen and lowered his voice so Duncan couldn't possibly overhear. "We never saw the person who attacked Dr. Fisher. In case he's still hanging around, I'd appreciate it if your officers could search the house and the grounds."

"He was found at the bottom of the cliff. What makes you think his attacker might be in the house?"

"In the basement, there's a passage that leads down to the caves by the shore."

"A secret passageway?" Chapman nudged his partner. "We gotta check that out."

Another squad car pulled up with lights flashing. Then two more unmarked vehicles. Though Blake hadn't expected such a large response, he was glad to see the cops converging on his front door. He'd meant what he said about a thorough search.

The man in charge wore a dark suit, white shirt and dark necktie. His hair was jet-black and curly. His ebony eyes held the haunted sadness of someone who had experienced recent tragedy. After he conferred briefly with Chapman, he introduced the plainclothes cop who was with him. "This is Detective Joe Curtis. I understand you have some concerns about an intruder."

"Yeah, I'm concerned." Blake shook hands with Curtis, a thick-necked man with a short-cropped, military haircut and shoulders like a bull. "I'm worried that whoever attacked Dr. Fisher is still here."

"Detective Curtis will be in charge of organizing a sweep of the house and the grounds." He held out his hand. "I'm Detective Andrei Lagios. Homicide."

Blake winced. "Is Dr. Fisher dead?"

"DOA at the nearest hospital."

"I'm sorry to hear that."

"Were you a close friend?"

Blake shook his head. "Hardly knew the man."

Teddy Fisher was, however, the person paying the bills for this restoration. Though Blake drew his necessary funds from an escrow account, Teddy's death would have an impact on what happened to the Manor and the lighthouse.

Those were worries for tomorrow. For right now, Blake had something else on his mind. He pulled Lagios aside. "Before you start taking statements, I need you to be aware of one thing. My son, Duncan, is autistic. I'm never sure how he'll react to strangers."

"I'll keep that in mind." His gaze sharpened. "Is there a reason I should talk to the boy?"

Blake considered lying to protect his son, but he was fairly sure that Lagios would see through any deception. Unlike the boyish Chapman, the homicide detective was intense. Tough. Professional. Though Andrei Lagios worked on a small-town police force, he sure as hell wasn't a hick.

"Earlier tonight," Blake said, "Duncan was outside playing. He was upset. Said a man grabbed his arm."

"The man who attacked Dr. Fisher?"

"Could be." That was truth. "Duncan said he didn't get a good look at the guy. Sometimes, he imagines things."

The detective gave a quick nod. "I'll try not to upset the boy. Why don't I talk to him first so he can go to bed?"

As if Duncan would fall asleep with all this commotion in the house. Blake led the way to the kitchen where he sat beside Duncan at the table, shielding him. His son concentrated intently on the coloring book, staying precisely within the lines.

When Lagios sat opposite them, Blake said, "Duncan, this is Detective Lagios."

Without looking up, Duncan said, "We tell the truth to the policemen."

Blake prompted, "Earlier today, you went outside to measure the yard for a baseball diamond. Then something happened. Tell us about it."

"Temperance was in the forest. She's my very, very best friend. She went close to the cliff. I'm not supposed to go there. Inappropriate behavior." He fell silent. The crayon in his hand poised above the page.

Blake guessed that Duncan had also gone to the edge of the cliff when he knew damn well he shouldn't. "It's okay, buddy. I'm not angry."

"I understand," Lagios said in a voice so gentle that it was almost musical. "Temperance went near the cliff. Then what?"

Duncan threw down the crayon. His fingers balled into tight little fists. "He grabbed me. And shook me. A bad man. He's very bad."

"What did he look like?"

"I don't know."

"It's okay," Lagios soothed. "Does he have a name?"

Duncan shouted. "Don't know."

Blake recognized the signs of an oncoming tantrum and

was glad when Madeline joined them. Her presence seemed to brighten the room and defuse the rising tension. She was so blessedly normal and grounded.

She introduced a clean-cut guy wearing a polo shirt and a sweater knotted around his neck, preppy-style. He looked familiar. "This is Grant Bridges, Assistant District Attorney. He's in charge of the T-ball program for the kids in town."

Bridges offered an affable grin as he shook hands with Blake. "I believe we've met. When you were staying at the Cliffside Inn."

"Of course." Blake recalled that Grant Bridges lived at the Inn. "Are you here in an official capacity?"

"I like to get in early on the investigation. This is going to be a high-profile homicide."

Blake recognized ambition when he saw it. Bridges was hoping to be assigned as prosecutor on this crime. "The detective had a few questions for my son."

"Madeline tells me that Duncan is interested in playing T-ball." He leaned toward the boy. "Is that right?"

Through pinched lips, Duncan said, "Yes."

"We'd be happy to have you on the team."

"I have gloves," Duncan said, too loudly.

"That's terrific." He glanced at Blake. "I'll make sure Madeline has our schedule."

When he looked back at her, his smile was warm and appreciative…too appreciative. His eyes twinkled.

Blake was pretty sure he didn't like Grant Bridges, and he had the sense that Lagios felt the same antipathy. Though the detective had acknowledged Bridges's presence, he retreated into stoic silence, waiting for the assistant DA to move aside so his investigation could proceed.

It was Madeline who provided the next distraction. To Duncan, she said, "Hey, I have a surprise for you."

He looked up at her. "Why?"

"Because I like you." She pulled her hand out of her pocket. Dangling from her fingertips was the shell necklace she'd found. "I thought you'd like this."

Lagios reacted. He stood so quickly that his chair crashed backward onto the floor. "Where did you find that?"

"In the caves." Her gaze stayed on Duncan. "You have that other shell that's exactly like these."

"From Temperance." Instead of reaching for the necklace, he plunged his hands into his lap. "Don't want to touch it."

"May I?" Lagios took the necklace from Madeline, handling it carefully by the string as if he didn't want to leave fingerprints.

"What is it?" Blake asked.

Instead of answering, Lagios spoke to Duncan. "Do you have another shell like these?"

The boy nodded.

"I'd like to see it."

"Fine," Madeline said. "Duncan, we'll go to your bedroom and find the shell."

Duncan climbed down from his chair. He walked close to Madeline without touching her. Under his breath, he counted every step as they left the kitchen.

As soon as they were gone, Blake confronted Lagios. "What is it? What's the deal with that necklace?"

"I've seen another exactly like this." His dark eyes turned as hard as anthracite. "The Seaside Strangler uses these necklaces to kill his victims."

Chapter Thirteen

Duncan went to find his seashell for the policeman with the sad, dark eyes. Madeline came with him, and he stayed close to her. Up the stairs to his bedroom. "One, two, three…"

These policemen were very loud. Some of them were mean. "…seven, eight…"

He put his hands over his ears so he couldn't hear the noise. He stared at the floor so he couldn't see, but the inside of his tummy hurt. There was something bad in the house. Something that could hurt him.

Inside his bedroom, Madeline closed the door. "They're making a lot of noise. Even more than the workmen on the roof. Does it bother you?"

"Some."

"They're searching the whole house to make sure we're safe. They're on this floor right now. With those heavy boots, it sounds like there are fifty of them."

"Not fifty." Fifty was half a hundred. Really a lot.

"Maybe five," she said.

In here with Madeline, he felt safe. Duncan ran across the floor and jumped into the center of his bed. The covers were soft and puffy. He wanted everybody to go away.

Madeline sat in the rocking chair beside his bed. "It's lucky that Mr. Bridges came here. He could be your baseball coach."

"I'm going to be a baseball player. Like Wade Boggs."

"Exactly like Wade Boggs." She rocked back and forth. He counted six times before she talked again. "Detective Lagios really wants to see your shell."

"He misses Sofia." Pretty Sofia in her long white dress. "He's unhappy."

"He might want to take the shell with him."

Inside his head, Duncan heard Temperance's voice. *She sells seashells…* "Danger."

"Where is the danger?"

"Basement." Like Temperance always said.

"Anywhere else?"

"Don't know." But he could feel it. All creepy and dark, it was coming closer. "I want my daddy."

"We can go back downstairs."

"No." His voice wasn't too loud. "I want him here."

Madeline frowned, but he knew she wasn't mad at him. She made that face when she was thinking. "I can get him, but I'd have to leave you here by yourself."

"Yes. I want him here. Here, here, here."

"Okay, I'll take the shell."

"No." He was louder. "I want Daddy."

"Stay right here. I'll be back in a flash."

When she left the room, he dove under the covers and curled up in a ball. Outside his room, he heard lots of feet walking. Policeman feet.

He couldn't hide under a blanket. That was dumb. And he didn't want to be a scaredy-cat. He was a baseball player. And he was brave.

He ran to his bedroom door and pulled it open. He charged into the hallway and ran smack into a big man in a suit.

"Hey, kid. Watch where you're going."

"You watch."

"Careful there. You're going to fall down."

Duncan turned away. He slipped.

The big man grabbed his hand. His skin was rough like a tree trunk. His breath was cold. Ice-cold.

"No." Duncan gasped. He couldn't breathe.

The big face came closer and closer. He had sharp, pointy teeth, and they were dripping with blood. Instead of arms, he had big heavy hammers.

They were in a dark, wet place. The hammer came down hard. "Don't hit me," he yelled.

He felt as if his bones were cracking.

Another thud from the hammer. He pulled his arms up over his head. "No, no, no. Help. Danger."

"What the hell is wrong with you, kid?"

He was a bully. A bad man.

Duncan fell to his knees. Thud, thud, thud. His eyes squeezed shut.

BLAKE HEARD his son's frantic cries and raced up the stairs to find Duncan curled up on the floor with Detective Curtis kneeling beside him. His beefy hand rested at Duncan's throat, feeling for a pulse.

He was touching Duncan. Damn it! Blake should have been more specific when he informed Lagios about his son's autism, should have warned him about touching.

He shoved Curtis's shoulder. "Get back."

The big cop looked up and shook his head in confusion.

"I don't know what happened. The kid came busting out of his room and ran right into me. I tried to steady him so he wouldn't fall down."

"Get away from him," Blake snapped.

He scooped Duncan off the floor and carried his limp body into his bedroom. Sitting on the bed, he held his son close. Duncan coughed. A sob convulsed his skinny chest and he clung tightly to his father.

"The bad man." Duncan choked out the words. "Hammer arms. And blood."

Blake looked past Duncan's shoulder to the doorway where Joe Curtis stood, watching and waiting. Though obviously nervous about what had happened, there was something menacing about the man. The way his fingers flexed then tightened into fists. The set of his heavy shoulders.

When Madeline touched Curtis's arm, he pivoted so quickly to face her that she took a step backward. He wasn't much taller than she, but his bulk loomed over her as she said, "It's best if you leave."

"What's wrong with the kid?" he asked.

Madeline stiffened her shoulders. As Blake well knew, she hated any suggestion that there was something wrong with his son. "Forget it, Detective. You wouldn't understand."

"I didn't do anything." He looked out toward the hall where a couple of other uniformed cops had gathered. "I swear. I didn't do a damn thing. The kid was just—"

"Frightened." Madeline's voice took on an authoritative teacherly tone as she defended his son. "Quite frankly, I can't blame Duncan. Not a bit. You're a big, rough man, Detective Curtis. In the eyes of a little boy, you must look as terrifying as a T-Rex."

There were guffaws from the cops in the hall.

Madeline silenced them with a glare. "Step back, gentlemen. We'll handle this."

When she again touched Curtis's arm to push him out of the way, he balked. In that physical contact, Blake saw a battle of wills. A stare-down. Behind her glasses, Madeline's eyes flared with determination.

Curtis met her gaze with an instant of unguarded hostility. Then he shrugged and stepped aside as Madeline closed the door to Duncan's bedroom and came toward them.

If Blake hadn't already been attracted to her, this moment would have convinced him that she was the right woman for him. She'd defended his son fiercely.

HOURS LATER, Madeline kicked off her slippers and dove under the bedcovers. The coolness of the sheets did little to quench her rising anxiety. Her mind raced. She remembered the impenetrable dark of the cave, the mangled body of Dr. Fisher, the clawing branches of trees as she ran through the forest toward the house. Most of all, she thought of Duncan.

The boy had been terrified after his encounter with Detective Curtis, and she knew in her heart that Duncan had sensed something. What was it? What did he see?

After Duncan had calmed down, Blake had stayed with him in his room, leaving her and Alma to deal with the herd of cops who centered their search on the passageway which definitely wasn't a secret anymore.

The police were reassuring, especially Detective Lagios. He seemed certain that the murder of Teddy Fisher was unrelated to the Manor. Teddy had a lot of enemies—one of whom he had driven over the edge.

Supposedly, they were safe. Madeline wasn't sure that she believed that logic. Any person capable of murder was dangerous. They might strike again.

She took off her glasses and reached to turn off her bedside lamp, then hesitated. Sleep wouldn't come easily tonight, not while her nerves vibrated with tension. Even though the Manor was locked up tightly, including the door from the basement leading into the house, and she had shoved her potted ficus against her bedroom door, she was still afraid.

She glanced at the novel on her bedside table—a thriller with a tough heroine who pulverized evil-doers with karate kicks. Nothing could be further from Madeline's reality. In her own way, she was tough. Growing up in foster care meant learning survival skills. But she'd never been a fighter.

There was a tap on the door. Blake whispered, "Madeline, are you awake?"

"Just a minute."

She leaped from the bed, dragged the ficus away from the door and opened it.

Exhaustion deepened the lines at the corners of his lips, but his hazel eyes burned with intensity. His gaze skimmed the outline of her body under her blue cotton nightgown. "I wanted to make sure you were all right," he said.

"I'm fine," she lied. "How's Duncan?"

"He seems okay. I'll never understand what goes on in that little head of his." He exhaled a weary sigh. "I've been watching him sleep for the past half hour."

Feeling exposed, she folded her arms across her breasts. For a moment, she considered grabbing her robe from the closet and covering up. Then she remembered his kiss, and she purposely lowered her arms to her sides. *Let him look. Let him come closer.* A night in his strong arms would be the perfect antidote to her fears.

She cleared her throat and asked, "Did Duncan tell you what he saw when he touched Detective Curtis?"

"A big, bad man with bloody teeth and hammer fists. Then, being Duncan, he started counting in Spanish and showed me how the hands on a clock move." He stepped inside her room, closed the door and glanced at the ficus. "Odd place to put a plant."

Not wanting to tell him that she'd been using her ficus to barricade the door, she ignored his observation. "I know you don't believe in psychic abilities, but we really must consider the possibility that Duncan sensed danger from Detective Curtis."

"Must we?" He raised an eyebrow. "Why?"

"Because Teddy Fisher was beaten to death."

"You think Curtis killed him?" He considered for a moment, then shook his head. "He's a cop, Madeline. His job involves danger. I'm not surprised that he gives off that vibe."

"Nobody knows Curtis well. Detective Lagios said he recently transferred here from Los Angeles."

"The LAPD? That's a tough place to work. A violent place. That's got to be what Duncan sensed."

She wasn't willing to dismiss Duncan's premonition so quickly. The boy had been right when Stuart Chapman had touched him and he had sensed that Stuart's wife was gravely ill. "What if Duncan is right? What if Curtis is dangerous?"

A smile curved his lips. "I get it, Madeline. You believe in Duncan."

"Of course I do."

"I appreciated the way you defended him when Curtis said there was something wrong with the kid." He reached toward her. With the back of his hand, he stroked the line of her chin. "But facts are facts. Duncan is autistic. He sometimes says things that don't make sense. He isn't like other kids."

In her mind, that was a positive attribute. Duncan was smarter than most. And more sensitive. "Being normal is highly overrated."

He came closer to her. "Are you speaking from experience?"

His voice had dropped to a low, intimate level. Even without her glasses, she could clearly see his intentions and she welcomed them. "I know what it's like to be an outsider."

"So do I."

She didn't believe for a moment that this tall, gorgeous, confident man had ever been the butt of jokes. Yet, he was diffident and cool. "Were you a bit of a lone wolf?"

"Even as a kid, I spent a lot of time by myself, imagining castles in the air."

She leaned toward him. The tips of her breasts were inches from his chest. "As an architect, you've been able to turn your daydreams into reality."

His arm slipped around her waist and pulled her close. "I usually get what I want."

Apparently, he wanted her. And she was glad, truly glad, because she wanted him, too. Willingly, she allowed herself to be overwhelmed by the force of his embrace and the wonderful pressure of his lips against hers. Joyfully, she savored the taste of him.

Behind her closed eyelids, starbursts exploded. Sensation flooded her body, rushing through her veins as his hand closed over her breast. His hard body pressed against hers. His thigh parted her legs.

An excited gasp escaped her lips. In her admittedly limited experience of lovemaking there had usually been a great deal of fumbling around. Not with Blake. He knew what he wanted. Even better, he knew what *she* wanted. Every murmur, every kiss, every caress aroused her more.

He was a fierce lover. Strong and demanding. How could she ever resist him? Why would she? Swept away by a roaring passion, she disregarded the small, logical voice in the back of her mind that told her this could never work, could never be a real relationship. They had no future. They were from different worlds. He was her employer. The bottom line she couldn't ignore: he was still in love with his late wife.

This might be a one-night stand. But what a night!

She tore at the buttons on his shirt. In a frenzy, their clothing peeled away. Naked, their bodies joined, and the impact stunned her. Her skin was on fire.

Every cell in her body throbbed with aching desire as he lowered her to the bed. His fingers tangled in her long hair, and he kissed her hard.

She clawed at his back, pulling him closer, needing him inside her. In the momentary pause while he sheathed himself in a condom, she couldn't keep her hands off him. His muscular arms. The crisp hair on his chest. The sharp angle of his jaw.

His gaze became tender. With an expression she'd never seen from him before, he looked deep, seeing her in a different way. Momentarily gentle, he stroked her cheek. "Your eyes are the most amazing color. Aquamarine."

He lightly tasted her lips. "I love your long hair."

He arranged her curls on the pillow, framing her face. Then he leaned down and kissed her again. The time for talk was over.

Chapter Fourteen

The next morning, Blake got out of his bed at the same time as usual. He followed his regular routine, got Duncan up and dressed. All the while, he knew that today was different—not because of the secret passageway in the basement or the police investigation or even the murder of Teddy Fisher. Today was different because of Madeline.

As he followed his son down the staircase, Blake had a bounce in his step. He couldn't wait to see her. His fingers twitched as he recalled the feel of her curly, silky black hair and the satin-softness of her ivory skin. The amazing color of her eyes made him think of deep, clear waters.

The intensity of her passion had surprised the hell out of him. Last night, Madeline had been a wild woman—an untamed, tempestuous force of nature. When he saw her this morning, he halfway expected her to growl. Or pounce. Oh yeah, that would be good.

As he stepped into the kitchen, his gaze went directly to her. Washing dishes at the sink, she had her back to him. Her luxurious hair was pulled into a tidy knot at the top of her head. Not one single, flirty tendril escaped. She'd covered her pastel-patterned cotton blouse and loose-fitting khaki slacks with a blue apron. On her feet were practical loafers, a little worn down at the heel. Definitely not the type of outfit worn by a wild woman. He'd been hoping for a topless sarong.

When she turned and faced him, her expression behind her black-rimmed glasses showed nothing more than the usual friendliness. Likewise, her smile was annoyingly calm.

"Good morning, Blake." She nodded to his son. "Hi, Duncan."

"Good morning," Blake said as Duncan climbed into his seat and began his silent breakfast-eating procedure.

Alma stalked toward him on four-inch heels. "Here's the deal, Blake. I know you hate when I make plans for you, but I had to set this appointment." With her pouffy hair, tight slacks and makeup, she was making ten times the effort to be attractive that Madeline put forth. She continued, "Detective Lagios will be here in about half an hour. He wants to finish the conversation you started last night."

"Fine," Blake said. His gaze returned to Madeline. Oddly enough, her prim exterior aroused him even more than if she'd been flaunting herself.

"I'll make fresh coffee for the detective," Alma said. "Maybe some sweet rolls. Would that be okay for your breakfast, Blake?"

"Whatever." Food was the last thing on his mind.

Alma turned to Madeline. "Did you know that Detective Lagios is single?"

"I wasn't aware," Madeline said.

"So is Grant Bridges. He's not a bad-looking guy and seems to have recovered from the tragedy of losing his bride on their wedding day."

"Must have been terrible," Madeline said.

Blake realized that she was avoiding his gaze, keeping herself so tightly wrapped that not even Alma suspected what had happened last night.

"I'll take breakfast in my studio," he said as he grabbed a mug of coffee. He needed to put some distance between himself and Madeline before he lost control.

In the studio, he sank into the chair behind his desk and quickly sorted through the progress reports of various crews and today's schedule. Concentrating on his work usually provided an orderly solution for life's other problems. No matter what else happened, he could see real progress in the completion of tasks.

Not today. He was distracted by Madeline's transformation. Today, she gave every appearance of propriety. Cool and distant. Nothing wanton about her. Was she playing games with him? Acting out a role? Was this prissy-proper attitude supposed to be a variation on the naughty-secretary fantasy?

He didn't think so. She wasn't a gamer. Madeline was just being herself, keeping her passions in check. But if he teased her, how would she react? Blake sipped his coffee. If he kissed her?

Lagios arrived before Blake's breakfast. After a brisk handshake, he took the chair opposite the desk. From his inner jacket pocket, he produced a small notebook. "I have a few more questions," he said.

"So do I." This conversation didn't need to be a confrontation; they were both on the same page. All the same, he would have appreciated an apology from Lagios for upsetting Duncan. "Starting with Detective Joe Curtis. I understand he's new in town."

"He's from LA. His experience has been useful on the Seaside Strangler investigation."

Blake thought of Madeline's concerns last night and her belief that Duncan had sensed a threat from Curtis. That suspicion could be easily erased if Curtis had an alibi for last night.

Blake tried to be subtle. "My son thought he recognized Curtis, but I don't recall meeting him. Has he ever been at the Manor before?"

"I don't know."

"What about last night? Was Curtis at the Manor last night or was he on duty?"

Lagios frowned. "What are you implying?"

So much for subtlety. "Does he have an alibi for the time of the murder?"

The detective's dark eyes flared with temper. "I don't keep track of the men I work with. When they're off duty, their time is their own. If you have questions about Curtis, I suggest you talk directly to him."

"I'll do that."

The door to the study opened, and Alma minced across the hardwood floor on her high heels. She carried a tray piled high with sweet rolls, bagels and a mug of coffee for Lagios. Her attempt at flirting with the detective fell flat as a water balloon dropped from a ten-story balcony.

Lagios didn't waste time with small-town charm. As soon as Alma left the room, he asked, "Have you noticed anyone unusual on the grounds of the Manor?"

"You'll have to be more specific," Blake said.

"You know what I mean."

Blake matched the detective's brusque manner with his own sarcasm. "If you're asking if I've seen obvious homicidal maniacs, the answer is no. But there are lots of people on the grounds, every day. I have several crews of workmen. Roofers. Carpenters. Painters."

"I'll need a list of names."

"Everything is taken care of through subcontractors. They hire their own men and pay them." He took a duplicate sheet from a folder inside his desk drawer. "These are the companies I'm working with."

"Did anyone have contact with Dr. Fisher?"

"I don't keep track of my crew." Blake lobbed Lagios's comment about Curtis back at him. "Off duty, their time is their own."

"How was your relationship with Fisher?"

"You suspect me? Seriously?" Blake's mood was moving rapidly from irritated to angry. "I have no motive for hurting Teddy Fisher. He's the guy who hired me—the man with the wallet. Plus, I have an alibi for last night."

"I had to ask." Without backing down, Lagios reached into his pocket and placed Duncan's shell on the desktop. "Your son can have this back."

"Did it match the necklace?"

Lagios nodded. "Necklaces similar to the one Madeline found were used by the Seaside Strangler."

The detective's sister, Sofia, had been one of the Strangler's victims. As Blake retrieved the shell and slipped it into his pocket, he adjusted his attitude and cut Lagios some slack. It must be hell to investigate the murder of a close family member. "Do you have any leads on the Strangler?"

"Not much." He glanced down at the notebook in his hand. "I brought my family here from New York to escape violence. I thought we'd be safe. Secure."

When he looked up, his abrupt manner was replaced by a haunted expression that Blake knew well. They had both suffered the loss of a loved one. They shared that pain.

"I feel the same way about Raven's Cliff," Blake said. "It seems like a good place for my son. Maybe here, in a small town, he won't be teased. The pace is slower. There's room to grow."

"Instead, you have a murder on your doorstep." Lagios frowned. "Then somebody like Curtis implies that there's something wrong with your boy. I'm sorry."

"Thanks." The air between them cleared. "The best way I can help your investigation is through Duncan. The person who grabbed him last night on the cliffs might be your murderer. Do you think it was the Strangler?"

"Not likely. The profile for Teddy's murder and the others is completely different."

"Unfortunately, Duncan doesn't respond to direct questions. And he has an active imagination." He decided against telling Lagios about his son's mention of Sofia. "Last night, he said that he saw Nicholas Sterling."

"The lighthouse keeper's grandson." Lagios sat up straighter. "Sterling has been dead for years."

And Blake sure as hell didn't want to start a rumor that his boy saw dead people. "I thought Duncan might have identified Nicholas Sterling from family portraits in the Manor. He might have noticed a resemblance."

"This is helpful. Gives us a starting place for a physical description." Lagios made a note. "Is there anything else Duncan mentioned?"

"Hammer hands," Blake said. "He kept talking about a man with pointy teeth and arms that were hammers."

The detective reached for his coffee mug and raised it

to his lips. He seemed to be struggling with a decision about how much to say and how much to leave blank. "I want to be able to trust you."

"We both want the same thing, Detective Lagios. To keep our families safe."

"I have the preliminary autopsy results." He looked directly into Blake's eyes, hiding nothing. "Teddy Fisher was beaten to death with a hammer."

DURING THE morning lessons with Duncan, Madeline tried to get him to open up about what he'd seen after touching Detective Joe Curtis, but the boy's thoughts scattered in a wild flurry, jumping from numbers to rhymes to simple repetitive motions. Nothing held his interest.

For the first time since she'd been at the Manor, she understood why Duncan had been diagnosed as autistic. He made no connection with her or anything she said. While she measured out geometrical shapes that usually fascinated him, Duncan hummed to himself and kicked his heel against the leg of his chair. He seemed lost in his own little world, unwilling to communicate.

She dropped her pencil. "It's much too nice a day to stay inside. Let's set out that baseball diamond."

He snapped to attention. "Outside."

"Yes, Duncan. We'll go outside. On the grass."

He whipped his baseball gloves from his pocket and made a beeline for the front door, counting every step.

Before leaving the house, she grabbed the duffel bag holding the bases and the measuring tape that Blake had provided for setting up a proper baseball field. As she trailed behind the small, determined boy, she couldn't help worrying about how she'd control him. If Duncan marched into the forest and approached the dangerous cliffs, she couldn't force him to stop, couldn't even touch him.

She dropped the duffel bag and loudly proclaimed, "Here is where we start with home plate."

Duncan halted, still facing the forest. In a singsong voice, he said, "She sells seashells."

"By the seashore," Madeline responded, hoping he'd turn around and come back toward her. "Duncan, come here. I need your help."

Slowly, he walked backward until he was beside her. "I want to play baseball."

"Let's set up the diamond."

"Really a square," he said.

For the next half hour, they measured and placed the bases, more or less in the right position. As long as she kept focus on the task, Duncan cooperated. But she was glad when Blake joined them.

Hearing his deep voice and seeing him stride toward them provoked a response much deeper than relief. Her stomach clenched. Her heartbeat accelerated. Though she was doing her best to maintain a proper attitude—as Duncan would say, appropriate behavior—she could barely control her raging hormones. She was willing to accept their lovemaking as a one-night stand, but she wanted so much more.

But she couldn't let her passion show. Not until she had a better idea of what their relationship—if it could even be called a relationship—entailed. Fortunately, she had a lifetime of experience in practicing restraint, never saying what she wanted, never complaining.

She was happy for the respite when he took control of their outdoor project, allowing her to step aside and watch as he and Duncan set up the bases and walked around them. First. Second. Third. Home.

"Again," Duncan shouted.

They walked again. Then jogged. Duncan's motor skills had improved tremendously.

Sitting on the duffel bag so she wouldn't get grass stains on her beige slacks, she admired Blake's easygoing attitude with his son. Male bonding, she thought. Athletics seemed to be a natural arena for fathers and sons.

With no tasks of her own, she was free to admire Blake himself. His long-legged gait. His masculine shoulders. His habit of pushing his overlong hair off his forehead. So incredibly handsome, he wasn't the type of man who usually gave her a second glance. She could hardly believe they'd made love last night with a passion as fiery as a supernova. Just thinking about it made her perspire.

Flapping her hand by her cheek, she fanned herself as she gazed up into the clear July sky. It was a warm day with the sun beating down. Several of the workmen hammering away at the Manor's rooftop had taken off their shirts.

Blake did the same. The sight of his bare chest and lean torso took her breath away. She had to make love to him again. There had to be at least one more night.

Her passionate reverie was interrupted by a car pulling up to the front door of the Manor. When she saw Detective Curtis emerge from the driver's side, she rose quickly and hurried toward him, hoping that she could handle this situation without disturbing Duncan and Blake.

Grant Bridges—dressed in a nicely tailored suit with a striped silk tie—stepped out of the passenger side and waved to her. "Hello, Madeline. Beautiful weather today."

She returned his friendly greeting. "How can I help you gentlemen?"

Curtis scowled, giving the impression that he was here under duress. "I wanted to check on the kid. Make sure he was okay."

"As well as can be expected," she said. "It's rather disruptive to have a murder so close to home."

His thick neck swiveled as he squinted toward the baseball diamond. He wore a blazer, probably to cover his shoulder holster, and a tie. Too many clothes for such a warm day. His forehead glistened with sweat. "Did the boy ever say anything? About why he got so freaked out?"

"What would you expect him to say?"

"Don't know." He stared at the field. "I should talk to him. Let him know that policemen aren't scary."

"Not today." She planted herself in front of him, ready to tackle him if he made a move toward Duncan. "Leave him alone."

"Good advice," Grant said. "Duncan seems to be doing okay. I hope you'll bring him to T-ball practice tomorrow. It'd be good for him to have other kids to play with."

"I couldn't agree more," Madeline said.

The smooth, charming Grant Bridges was the direct opposite of the thuggish policeman. With an easy grin, he asked, "Will you be coming with Duncan to T-ball practice?"

"Of course."

"Maybe afterward, we could get a cup of coffee."

He was asking her for a date? Amazing! There had been times in her adult life when she'd gone months without any man noticing she existed. Now, she had two very eligible bachelors who were both interested. Obviously, she should have moved to Maine a lot sooner.

But it wasn't right to lead him on. "I'm sorry, Grant. My responsibilities with Duncan are keeping me so busy that I can't make other plans."

"I'd like to be friends." A hint of sadness tugged at his smile. "Sometimes it's hard for me to talk to the locals. They look at me, and they remember the tragedy."

"You have my deepest sympathy." She remembered stories about the accident, in which Grant's bride was swept off the cliff on their wedding day. How could anyone get over such a terrible tragedy? He probably wasn't even asking for a date. Just companionship.

"They never found her. Camille could still be alive." He straightened his shoulders. "I want to move on, but I can't."

She changed the topic. "How's the murder investigation going?"

"I hate to say this, but suspicion seems to be centered on Mayor Wells. He was the last person to see Dr. Fisher alive. And he had motive."

Curtis cleared his throat. "We shouldn't talk about the ongoing investigation."

"No point in trying to keep this a secret. Everybody in town knows what's going on. Perry Wells hated Fisher."

"Why?" she asked.

"You might have heard about anonymous letters to the press about corruption in the mayor's office. Those accusations were written by Teddy Fisher."

She found it hard to believe that the mayor was capable of the violence that had killed Dr. Fisher. His injuries had been brutal. "Political accusations come with the territory for any elected official. They don't seem like a motive for murder."

"The mayor has been under a lot of pressure. He's falling apart. I hardly know him anymore." The smile slipped from his face. "A damned shame. Perry Wells was almost my father-in-law."

Again, she said, "I'm so sorry, Grant."

"Camille was an amazing woman. I miss her. I miss the family we could have had together." His gaze returned to the grassy field. "A son. Like Duncan."

As if sensing Grant's scrutiny, Duncan waved.

"Excuse me," Grant said. "I need to see what the newest member of my T-ball team wants."

He jogged toward Duncan and Blake, leaving her alone with Joe Curtis. When the policeman took a step to follow, she snapped, "Don't."

"Why not? Give me a reason."

Because she didn't want Duncan to be frightened again and she'd lay down her life to protect him. "I don't want you near him."

When he confronted her directly, she realized just how big he was. His shoulders looked massive enough to haul a Volkswagen.

His mouth curled in a sneer. "Why the hell shouldn't I talk to the kid?"

"Because you frighten him." She remembered his earlier question; Curtis was afraid that Duncan had said something about him.

She had no intention of explaining Duncan's abilities to this man. All she wanted was to deflect his focus from the boy. "The boy doesn't know anything, but I do."

She saw a flicker of wariness in his eyes. "Yeah? And what do you know?"

Though she'd never been a good liar, she summoned up all her confidence and nerve. This lie was for a good cause. To protect Duncan.

"I'm a little bit psychic," she said. "I can see your aura. So much violence. So much rage."

Though he scoffed, she could tell that her words made an impact. "You're a violent man, Joe Curtis." Possibly that was why he'd left the LAPD. She continued, "I know why you're here in Raven's Cliff. I'm warning you. Stay away from Duncan. Or I'll tell everything."

"You're bluffing."

"Maybe." She refused to break eye contact. "Maybe not."

Grant jogged up beside her. His earlier sadness vanished behind a brilliant smile. "Duncan is definitely on the team."

Abruptly, Joe Curtis pivoted, ending their face-to-face confrontation. He lumbered around the car to the driver's side and opened the door. Before he got behind the wheel, he cocked his fingers like a gun and aimed it at her. "I'll be seeing you, Madeline."

She wasn't looking forward to the next time.

Chapter Fifteen

Madeline went to bed early that night. During the course of the day, she and Blake had exchanged only a few words. Neither of them had mentioned their previous night of passion. Nor did they speak of what would happen next.

A few times, she'd caught him watching her with what she hoped was longing. Or perhaps, curiosity. She couldn't tell what was going on inside his head. Just like his son, Blake revealed very little of himself. The only thing he'd been adamant about was a restoration project he'd started in one of the upstairs bedrooms that involved some delicate handiwork. Repeatedly, he'd told them that no one was allowed to enter that room.

Though he'd given her no real reason to believe that he might show up at her bedroom door, she dressed in her best pink satin nightshirt with matching panties—a gift to herself from one of the better lingerie shops in Boston. With her long hair brushed to a glossy sheen, she slipped between the sheets and waited.

Duncan had been tucked in half an hour ago, plenty of time for him to be sound asleep. If Blake intended to join her in bed, there should be nothing stopping him.

A glance at the bedside clock told her that it was exactly four minutes since the last time she'd checked the time. She ought to take matters into her own hands. Trot down the hall to his room.

Their passion last night had been spectacular. Of that, she had no doubt. But he might not want a repeat. He might have decided that it was inappropriate to seduce his son's tutor. Or he might be remembering his beloved Kathleen. An angel. How could anyone compete with such a perfect memory?

Another ten minutes ticked slowly by. She exhaled a frustrated sigh. *He wasn't coming.* Might as well shove the ficus against the door and try to sleep.

Then she heard a rap on her bedroom door. She bolted to a sitting posture on the bed and called out, "Come in."

"You come out," Blake responded.

In the ensuing silence, the pounding of her heart was louder than the drum and bugle corps in the St. Patrick's Day Parade. *He wanted her to come to him.*

She floated from the bed to the mirror, put on her glasses to check her reflection, then took them off. Her hazy vision matched her dreamlike mood as she wafted to the door and opened it.

A trail of colorful wildflowers—daisies and bluebells—led down the hallway, marking the way from her bedroom to his. Never had she expected such a sweet gesture. Step by step, she gathered her bouquet, pausing at the slightly opened door to Duncan's bedroom and peeking inside at the soundly sleeping child.

Like a bride to the altar, holding her colorful bouquet, she walked the few paces. No matter what else happened between them, she would always remember this moment. More than passion, he had given her romance.

When she pushed open the door to Blake's room, she found him waiting. He scooped her off her feet and into his arms, neatly closing his door at the same time.

Her flowers scattered across the sheets as he deposited her on his bed. Unlike last night's wild frenzy of passion, tonight was slow. Deliberate. Divine.

She savored his kisses. Pushing aside his unbuttoned shirt, she traced the muscles on his chest. His strong but gentle caresses pulled her so close that they breathed as one being. Their hearts synchronized in perfect harmony.

Through her swirling senses, she heard a cry.

It was Duncan. "Danger," he shouted. "Danger."

INSTANTLY, Blake responded to his son's voice. He leaped from the bed and charged down the hall to Duncan's room. The door was shut when it should have been open. He yanked the knob, flung it open and stormed inside.

His son stood on his bed, cowering against the headboard. As Blake approached, Duncan jumped toward him, into his arms. He was cold, shivering.

"What happened?" Blake asked. "Bad dream?"

"Bad dream. Bad man. Bad dream."

Blake stroked Duncan's fine blond hair. "It's okay, buddy. Nobody is going to hurt you."

"I saw his shadow. Hammer hands."

It had been several months, nearly a year, since Duncan had last been yanked awake by a nightmare. After his mother died, these bad dreams came almost every night, but that behavior was history. Until now.

Blake glanced toward Madeline as she entered the room, wearing that sexy satin nightshirt that showed off her long, curvy legs. Her flushed complexion and disheveled hair contrasted with her calm voice as she asked, "What should I do? Duncan, do you want a glass of water?"

"No," Duncan shouted. "He'll get you. Stay."

Blake sat on the edge of the bed with Duncan on his lap. "The nightmare is gone. We're all safe."

When Madeline sat beside them—carefully not touching his son—her presence felt right. They were a unit. Together, they faced the dark fears in Duncan's mind.

She urged, "Tell us what happened, Duncan. Everything you can remember."

"Noise," he said.

"You heard a noise," she prompted.

"Thump. Big feet. The door opened up. Opened up. Opened up wide. Shadows came inside. A big shadow." He shook his head. "Danger."

"But your door was closed," Blake said.

"He shut it." His shoulders slumped as he began to calm down. "All gone now. All gone."

Blake cradled his son against his bare chest. This sure as hell wasn't the way he had planned to spend this night, but Duncan came first. And he knew Madeline would agree with him. "You've got nothing to worry about, buddy."

Duncan pulled away and looked into his eyes. It was unusual for the boy to make such direct contact. His voice was normal without a hint of agitation. "Daddy, I saw him. I really saw him."

"Who? Who did you see?"

"The man."

"What did he look like?"

"He smelled like the ocean."

Had this been more than a nightmare? It was possible that someone had crept up the staircase and into his son's room. Blake needed to know. "Concentrate, buddy. Tell me about the man. Was he tall?"

Duncan frowned and looked down at his hands. He laced his fingers together, then pulled them apart. After three repetitions of this gesture, he murmured, "She sells seashells."

Last night, Duncan had been approached on the cliff by a stranger—someone had grabbed his shoulder. Duncan was a witness. He might have seen the man who murdered Teddy Fisher. "Duncan, look at me."

The boy clapped his hands together. "All gone."

Damn, this was frustrating. All Blake wanted was an answer to a simple question. "Does the man have a name?"

"Time for sleep, Daddy." He wriggled out of Blake's arms and dove under his covers. "Nighty-night, Madeline. Don't let the bedbugs bite."

Duncan's fears—having been expressed—seemed to disappear. He closed his eyelids. With each calm breath, his skinny chest rose and fell in an untroubled, steady rhythm.

Blake was nowhere near so calm. He whispered to Madeline. "I'm staying here until he's asleep."

"Of course." She left the room.

Settling into the rocking chair beside the bed, Blake fastened the buttons on his shirt. He hoped Duncan's vision had only been a nightmare, but feared otherwise.

What the hell should be done? Trust the cops to take care of things? Though Detective Lagios seemed like a competent officer, his abilities were limited. The only clue Duncan could offer was to say he'd seen a bad man. Or Nicholas Sterling, who had been dead for years.

The Raven's Cliff police force didn't have enough manpower to stand guard over the Manor day and night.

Even if they could, there was no sure protection against a determined assailant. There were dozens of ways into this sprawling house. Windows that were being replaced. Doors that were off the hinges. Installing a security system was a waste of time with all the workmen coming and going. Not to mention the secret passageway that led from the caves into the basement.

If Duncan truly was in danger, they should pack up and leave Raven's Cliff. But Duncan was doing well in this place. Just this afternoon, they'd played baseball like a regular father and son.

Moving carefully so he wouldn't wake Duncan, Blake slipped out of the room into the hallway.

Madeline popped through her bedroom door where she'd obviously been waiting. Wearing her flannel bathrobe with her glasses perched on her nose and her hair tied back at her nape, she gave the clear signal that she wasn't interested in sex.

"Is Duncan okay?" she whispered.

He nodded and pointed toward the staircase. Together, they descended and went into the kitchen.

She went to the cabinets by the sink. "I could really use a cup of tea."

"I was thinking of something stronger." From a top shelf, he took down a bottle of bourbon and poured a couple of shots into a tumbler. "You?"

"I'll stick to chamomile." She placed the teakettle on the burner and turned up the flame.

He took a sip and savored the burn. "Duncan hasn't had a nightmare like this in months."

"I can't blame him for being upset. It's been a rough couple of days." Her gaze rested on the poster board—

Duncan's Schedule. "Being lost in the woods. The murder. His reaction to Joe Curtis."

"He's agitated. Overexcited."

"Of course."

Blake really wanted to believe that his son's nightmare was nothing more than imagination—a disturbing sleep experience. He sank into a chair and took another drink. "What if he really saw someone?"

"It's possible. Very possible." She dove into the chair opposite him and leaned forward on her elbows. Her robe gaped open, giving a glimpse of the pink satin. "Someone could have come into his room."

Fear struck him hard. "A killer in the same room with my son."

Behind her glasses, her eyes shone with purpose and hope. "It's up to us, Blake. We have to find out what Duncan saw."

He agreed, but trying to figure out what was going on in Duncan's brain was like entering a maze. "Got any ideas?"

"There's got to be a way we can get Duncan to identify the person who grabbed him on the cliff."

"Then what?" He inhaled another gulp of bourbon, hoping to deaden the fear that writhed inside his chest. "I won't put my son through the ordeal of testifying. He can hardly stand to be in the same room with other people much less face a judge and jury. Damn it, he's only six years old."

"We need to know the truth, Blake."

"Here's what I need, Madeline. To keep my child safe. I should cancel all the work crews and bar the doors. Better yet, we should leave. Get the hell away from this cursed little town."

On the stove, the teakettle whistled, and she went to prepare her drink. "Is that what you want, Blake? To leave?"

"No." His response was immediate and definite. He was enjoying the restoration of this American Federalist estate, especially the project he'd started in the upstairs bedroom this afternoon. Even more important, Duncan's behavior improved every day by leaps and bounds. "I want my son to have a normal life, to play baseball. I want him to have a chance to be like other kids."

She returned to her seat opposite Blake and placed the flower-sprigged cup and saucer on the tabletop. "That's not too much to hope for."

Ever since the first diagnosis of autism, Blake's life with Duncan had been a series of disappointments. He'd learned not to expect too much. A normal life? "It's an impossible dream."

Reaching across the table, she laced her fingers with his. Her hand was soft and warm from holding her teacup. "Sometimes," she said, "the impossible comes true."

Her sincerity struck a chord inside him. Through his anger and frustration, he felt an echo of her hope. Sometime. Somehow. Someday. His son would be all right.

"I want to believe that."

"You can."

He liked the way her common sense cut through all the complications. She made all things seem possible. In so many ways, she amazed him. Being with Madeline was part of the reason he wanted to stay in Raven's Cliff. Their relationship was still in the early, delicate stages. He needed time to nurture his feelings for her, to see if his heart could ever blossom again.

But Duncan came first. "I've got to protect my son. If he's in danger, we can't stay here."

"As you well know," she said, "I'm Duncan's biggest

advocate. I think he sees things that the rest of us don't. But what happened tonight might have been nothing more than a bad dream."

"True." He could be making too much of a nightmare. "If we stay, we can't leave him alone. Not for a minute."

"But we can't lock him up in his room. Tomorrow, we should go to the T-ball practice in town."

"That's dangerous on so many levels. First, there's the basic problem of having Duncan interact with other kids. Leaving the house. Changing his schedule." A worse thought occurred. "What if he sees the killer?"

"A good thing," she said firmly. "If he identifies the killer, Lagios can arrest him. Duncan will be safe."

She made the process of putting his son in close proximity to a murderer sound rational. "The next thing you'll suggest is that we arrange for a police lineup of the main suspects."

"Probably not," she conceded. "That's too much pressure. I wouldn't want to put Duncan in the position of coming face-to-face with his nightmare man."

With a final squeeze, she withdrew her hand and concentrated on her tea. Her ladylike manner when she lifted the cup to her lips was a definite turn-on. He was tempted to sweep everything off the kitchen table and take her right here.

"Perhaps," she said, "there's a way for Duncan to see the suspects without facing them. We could arrange our own lineup."

"How?"

"Using your cell phone, you could take photos of the various suspects. I believe the police are concentrating on the mayor, Perry Wells."

"I still don't understand what you're talking about."

"We can make it a game. Like a lesson plan. Show Duncan all the photos and watch his reaction."

Once again, she'd come up with a simple solution for a complex problem. Using cell-phone photos, they could create their own photo array for Duncan to use in identification. In that way, his son wouldn't have to face the police. If he recognized the killer, they'd be right there beside him.

Blake turned the idea over in his head, looked at it from several angles. He couldn't find a flaw.

He raised his tumbler to her in toast. "We'll do it. It's a good plan."

"Thank you." She clinked her dainty teacup with his bourbon tumbler.

A very good plan. Maybe even brilliant. If grade-school teachers were running Homeland Security, the terrorists wouldn't stand a chance.

Chapter Sixteen

"First base, second base…" In the back of the car, Duncan counted to himself and punched his batting glove into the big catcher's mitt. Yesterday, Daddy had showed him how to do a high five. "…third base. Home plate. Home run."

He was on a team. A T-ball team. And he knew all the numbers. He leaned forward against his seat belt and stuck out his catching glove toward the front seat. "Madeline. High five."

She turned around and slapped the glove. "High five."

She looked funny in her Red Sox baseball cap with her ponytail hanging out the back. But her teeth were pretty and white, and she smiled a lot. That made him think of his best friend, Temperance, and how it sounded when she laughed. He wished Temperance could see him play baseball.

His Daddy parked and turned around. He smiled, too.

"Hey, buddy."

"Hey, Daddy."

"I'm proud of you, Duncan. Let's play ball."

He jumped out of the car. There was a fence and a green field with bases. Lots of kids. Lots of parents.

Duncan wasn't scared. He knew all the numbers.

STEPPING OUT of the car into a sunny summer day, Madeline tensed. The possibility of running into the person who killed Teddy Fisher was secondary to her concerns for Duncan. More than anything, she wanted him to have a positive experience this afternoon. She walked stiffly at Blake's side—as apprehensive as if she herself were approaching the batter's box in Fenway Park.

The baseball diamond where the kids—aged five to seven—played T-ball was in a park across the street from the high school. A tall chain-link fence formed the backstop. The grass was cut short in the infield, and the paths for base running were marked off with white chalk lines. A simple setup with no dugouts or bleachers. She noticed that some of the other adults had brought along their own lawn chairs.

Grant Bridges sauntered toward them. His casual shorts and T-shirt didn't flatter him nearly as much as his suit and tie. Though he seemed fit, he lacked the athletic grace that came so naturally to Blake.

"Glad you're here," Grant said as he shook hands with Blake and twinkled a grin at Madeline. "With Duncan playing we've got enough kids for two full teams."

"Nine players on a team," Duncan said quickly.

"That's right," Grant said. "Come with me and we'll meet the other kids."

With a wave of his gloved hand, Duncan went forward. Madeline held her breath. Since she'd never seen Duncan with other children, she didn't really know what to expect. But Blake did. With arms folded across his chest and every muscle in his body clenched, he radiated nervous energy.

They were close enough to overhear the other kids greet

Duncan. He was quickly surrounded by four boys and two girls, all wearing baseball caps.

A stocky, redheaded boy who looked as if he might belong to the Chapman clan said, "You live in that big place near the lighthouse."

"Yes," Duncan said.

"There was a murder there."

The other kids jostled closer, obviously curious. There were comments about scary murders and the curse. One of the boys spat into the dirt.

Madeline noticed that Blake's arms had dropped to his sides and he leaned forward on the balls of his feet as if ready to immediately sprint to his son's aid.

The redheaded kid spoke to Duncan again. "Did you see him? Did you see the dead guy?"

"No."

A skinny little girl with long blond braids started to tremble. "Don't talk about it. I'm scared."

"Geez, Annie," said the other girl. "You're such a big crybaby."

"Am not!"

With his gloved hand, Duncan reached toward Annie and patted her shoulder. "It's okay. The bad man isn't here."

"Aren't you scared?"

"Sometimes." He shrugged. "I don't like T-Rex dinosaurs."

"Me, too," piped up the shortest boy in the group. "And sharks. I hate sharks. They can eat you up in one bite."

Grant stepped in to break up the conversation, assigning them places in the field for practice. Duncan ran to second base and stood on the bag. Though his lips were tight, Madeline detected the beginning of a grin. She beamed back at him. A sense of real pride bubbled up inside her. When Grant lobbed a ball toward him, Duncan managed to scoop it up and throw in the general direction of first base. His playing skills seemed to be no better and no worse than most of the other kids'.

She touched Blake's arm. "He's going to be okay."

"Thanks to you." When he looked at her, his eyes held a special tenderness and intimacy. "You've done so much. Our little family is coming together."

Our family? He seemed to be including her in that unit. "We're a good team."

"You, me and Duncan," he said. "I never imagined my son being able to play baseball."

She held his gaze, not wanting to make too much of the casual way he lumped them together. Being accepted as part of a family—his family—was deeply important to her. She'd always yearned for a family of her own. Not her adoptive parents. Not her addict mother who'd tossed her into the foster-care system. Certainly not her genetic sibling, Marty. Which reminded her that she still hadn't found the right time to tell Blake about the diamond theft. Now was certainly not that moment.

She turned toward the sidelines where the other parents had gathered. "We should introduce ourselves to the parents of Duncan's new friends."

"Friends," he said with obvious satisfaction. "Duncan's friends. That's a hell of a concept."

"Maybe we can set up a couple of playdates."

He took his cell phone from his pocket. "Or snap a

couple of pictures. I'm going to include Grant Bridges in our photo array."

She didn't understand why he'd taken such a dislike to Grant. "Okay."

None of the people they met seemed the least bit suspicious. Average people. Very pleasant. Like the kids on the field, they were all buzzing about the murder of Teddy Fisher. The general opinion seemed to be that Dr. Fisher was an obnoxious person, too rich for his own good, a genuine eccentric.

"And dangerous," said Lucy Tucker in a conspiratorial tone. Her trinket shop—Tidal Treasures—was in the center of town, and Lucy seemed to have her finger on the pulse of Raven's Cliff.

"Why dangerous?" Madeline asked.

The petite strawberry blonde pulled her aside. "You didn't hear this from me, but Dr. Fisher's experiments at his lab caused the epidemic. You know, the dark-line disease that killed people? If it hadn't been for Dr. Peterson, we'd all be dead."

With no encouragement, Lucy rattled on about the lady doctor who had apparently hooked up with a sexy toxicologist and they were getting married. "I mean, he's a babe magnet. And a doctor."

Madeline had never been fond of gossip but wanted to bond with Lucy, who was the aunt of Annie—the little girl with braids whom Duncan had comforted. "About the epidemic," she said. "Weren't there anonymous letters in the paper saying that Mayor Wells was to blame?"

"Lower your voice," Lucy warned as she nodded toward her left. "That skinny guy in the suit is Rick Simpson, the mayor's top aide."

Rick Simpson appeared to be deep in conversation with two other men who looked as if they'd just stepped out of their offices. "Who's with him?"

"A couple of guys who work in the D.A.'s office. You know, lawyers."

Madeline glanced toward the baseball diamond where Grant Bridges was organizing the kids into two teams, then turned back to Lucy. "There are a lot of high-powered people here. Are they all parents?"

"Mostly," Lucy said. "Some of them are here because the mayor's wife supports the baseball program."

Apparently, showing up at a T-ball game was a good way to impress the powers that be. Now Madeline understood why Grant Bridges—a single man with no children of his own—had volunteered to coach the team. This was his way of making contacts. "Why is Beatrice Wells so involved?"

"Raven's Cliff baseball is a whole program—from these little ones to middle school. According to Beatrice, sports are a good way to keep the kids off the street."

These teams of five- to seven-year-olds hardly looked like budding juvenile delinquents, but Madeline liked the idea of children being involved in group sports, especially during the summer when they tended to lose focus. From her years of teaching, she remembered how dreadful the first weeks of school could be.

But she wasn't here to discuss her educational philosophy with Lucy. Madeline returned to the pertinent gossip about the murder. "I've heard that Mayor Wells is a suspect."

"If he killed Teddy Fisher, I say good for him. Fisher was a menace." Her blue eyes brightened as she caught sight of two tough-looking fishermen approaching. "That's my boyfriend, Alex Gibson. Got to run."

Madeline turned her gaze toward the field where Duncan's team sat in a row on the sideline, waiting for their turn to bat. The rules in T-ball were different than regular baseball. Though one of the kids stood on the mound, the pitcher didn't really throw the ball. He just pantomimed the motion. The actual ball rested on a stand, and the batter had unlimited swings in trying to hit it. An inning came to an end when every kid on the team had had a turn at bat.

The theory was to give the kids an idea of how to run bases and field without really keeping score. The atmosphere should have been low-pressure, but Blake was tense as he came up beside her. "Duncan is next."

"He'll do fine," she assured him.

"We haven't practiced much on batting. I showed him how to swing, but that's about it."

The batter before Duncan wound up and unleashed a monster swing that spun him around like a top. He did, however, miss the ball standing on the tee.

"Strike one," his teammates yelled.

His second swing connected for a dribbling little hit that was enough for the boy to run to first base.

It was Duncan's turn. As he walked to the plate, his lips were moving. Madeline knew he was silently counting his steps. His small gloved hands wrapped around the bat, and he took his stance. With serious concentration, he swung. A hit!

"*Yes,*" Blake said with a quiet fist pump. "Okay, son. Now run. Run to first."

Duncan went to first. Then second. That was where he

stopped. Breathing hard, he gave a high five to the second baseman for the other team. Then he waved to his father.

"That's my boy. He hit a double."

While Duncan was on base, Blake concentrated on the field with a mixture of pride and incredulity. He couldn't believe how well Duncan was doing. No outbursts. No signs of rising panic. The batting gloves kept him shielded from unwanted touches, and the mechanics of the game kept his attention occupied. When he crossed home plate, he jumped on it with both feet.

Even more satisfying for Blake was the way Duncan interacted with his teammates. Though his son never laughed, a tiny grin played around the corners of his mouth. Blake overheard Duncan volunteering information, citing statistics about Madeline's beloved Red Sox.

Even that jerk, Grant Bridges, took notice of Duncan's expertise. "You're quite a Sox fan," he said.

"Yes," Duncan replied. "And the Cubbies."

That's my boy!

Blake's paternal reverie ended abruptly when he saw Helen Fisher charging toward him from the street. She was dressed in black from head to toe in apparent mourning for her dead brother. She'd topped the outfit with a big-brimmed straw hat that made her look like a walking lampshade.

She planted her feet in front of him and glared. "I want an accounting of every penny you spend on the restoration of the Manor. And I want it now."

Blake had no intention of being drawn into a business discussion at his son's T-ball game. "My condolences on the loss of your brother."

"Right. Thanks." She spat the words. "Teddy died without a will and has no heirs. That means Beacon Manor now belongs to me."

"That's for the probate courts to decide."

"Don't you dare put me off." Her voice rose to a finger-nails-on-chalkboard vibrato. "I own it."

Madeline stepped in to defuse the situation. "Perhaps we could talk about this another time."

Helen's furious glare swept past her and encompassed the rest of the people gathered at the sidelines. "I own the Manor and the lighthouse. I might just decide to move in and shut down the renovations entirely."

A tough-looking guy growled at her. "You can't do that."

"Don't tell me what I can't do, Alex Gibson."

"The lighthouse has to be repaired," he said. "It's the only way to lift the curse."

"All of you fishermen are so superstitious." Her mouth puckered. "The Manor is a historic landmark. The curse isn't real."

As Alex Gibson rose to his feet, Blake recognized him. He was the fisherman whom Duncan had seen at the docks and reacted to—definitely someone Blake should have in his photo array of suspects.

"Never deny the curse," Alex said darkly.

The little strawberry blonde who owned the trinket shop backed him up. "Helen, please. We're on the right track with repairing the lighthouse."

"How can you say that? Teddy was killed." Amid the crowd who were mostly dressed in summery clothing, her black dress marked her as a harbinger of bad luck. "You'd all better get used to treating me with more respect. I'm a wealthy woman now."

Which sounded to Blake like a damn good motive for

murder. Did Helen have the strength to beat her brother to death with a hammer?

Beatrice Wells hurried toward them, covering the last few yards across the grass with surprising speed for a small, short-legged woman. Gasping for breath, she said, "Helen, dear, you simply must lower your voice. You're upsetting the children."

Was she? Blake glanced back toward the field. None of the kids were watching. Even Duncan appeared to be undisturbed as he stared across the baseball diamond at the far edge of the outfield.

"Of all people," Helen said to Beatrice, "I'd expect you to understand. The money my brother threw away by hiring a world-famous designer could have gone to charity."

Beatrice tossed an apologetic smile toward Blake while Helen continued, "My brother got rich, and I spent my whole life struggling to get by."

"Not much of a struggle," said the trinket-shop owner. "The way I've heard it, you own your house and your bills are paid by a family trust."

Mayor Perry Wells had followed his wife to the sidelines. Though he was obviously ragged around the edges and stressed, his voice rang with the authority of his office. "Everyone calm down. You're distraught, Helen. Which is understandable under the circumstances. But you need to take it easy."

"Or what? What are you going to do, Perry?" She sneered. "Are you going to kill me, too?"

Beatrice gasped. Her small hand flew to cover her mouth. A murmur ripped through the people at the sidelines.

Helen took no notice. She turned on her heel and stalked off.

To his credit, Perry Wells didn't react to Helen's accusation. He pasted a smile on his face. "It's a beautiful day. Beautiful! Play ball."

Though Blake took out his cell phone and started snapping picture of possible suspects, he had to agree with the mayor. A beautiful day!

Raven's Cliff was one hell of a weird little town, but his son was thriving. This T-ball game was as close to normal as Duncan had been in years.

Madeline came up beside him. "How are you doing?"

"Normal." He savored the word. Nothing in the world seemed more beautiful than an ordinary day, watching Duncan at play with other kids. No tantrums. No hysterics. No inappropriate behavior.

"Helen Fisher didn't get to you?"

"Not at all."

It would take more than wild-eyed demands and accusations from Helen Fisher to drive him away. This little town was where Blake intended to stay. In spite of the curse.

Chapter Seventeen

During the four innings of T-Ball, Blake had collected a series of photos on his cell phone which he printed out in his office and spread across his desktop. None of these faces struck him as the visage of a murderer. He glided his hands above the pictures, trying to pick up a vibe, an idea of who among them might be dangerous. He closed his eyes and did it again. Nothing. Not even a tremor.

How did Duncan feel when he sensed danger? Did his pulse accelerate? Were there images? The boy talked about sounds. The thud of a hammer. The slam of the door.

In the past, Blake had dismissed his son's reactions, considering them to be imaginary. Preparing this photo array was the closest he'd come to acknowledging the possibility that his son had some kind of psychic ability. Though Blake wanted to tell himself that the pictures were only a police lineup to jog Duncan's memory, he knew it was more. Duncan saw more than other people; he sensed moods and the past history of people he touched. Was that better or worse than a diagnosis of autism?

Blake sprawled in his desk chair. Tilting back, he stared at the ceiling. A couple of the roofers were still hammering, though it was after five o'clock. Time for Duncan's dinner.

The T-ball game had thrown their schedule off. By damn, that disruption was worth it. The couple of hours they'd spent on the baseball diamond would always be a treasured memory. Duncan's first hit. His first time around the bases. In his batting gloves, Duncan had been part of the group—just like any normal six-year-old. It didn't matter if he was psychic or hypersensitive or autistic. He was happy.

Madeline came through the open door of his office. Her cheeks were slightly sunburned from being outside this afternoon, and she looked particularly vivacious as she scanned the photo array. "This doesn't exactly look like murderer's row, does it?"

"They all seem pretty average," he said. "Where's Duncan?"

"In the kitchen with Alma, having dinner." She picked up the photo of the mayor. "Perry Wells. I hope it's not him. The poor man has gone through enough tragedy. He didn't have time to get over losing his daughter on her wedding day before the epidemic hit Raven's Cliff. Now, he has to deal with anonymous letters to the newspaper, accusations and gossip."

"All of which might have driven him over the edge, turning a basically decent man into a killer."

"Do you think that's possible?" Behind her glasses, her eyes were troubled. "Can a truly good person be driven to commit a terrible crime?"

"There's plenty of times when I've been angry enough or frustrated enough to consider murder."

"But you didn't act on that impulse," she pointed out.

"Thinking violent thoughts is different from carrying them out. I've always been puzzled by the nature versus nurture issue."

"Genetics," he said.

"Is behavior predetermined by DNA?" She frowned. "Is someone born to be bad? Or is that a learned behavior?"

"It sounds like you're thinking of someone specific."

"My brother, Marty."

It was the first time she'd spoken of her family, and he sensed that this was important to her. "Younger brother or older?"

"About two years older than me. He was always very handsome. We don't look much alike, expect that we're both tall and have big, gawky feet."

"There's nothing wrong with your feet." His gaze scanned from her ponytail to the tips of her sneakers. "I like *everything* about your body. Your long legs. Your slim torso. Your—"

"I get it," she said, interrupting his listing of her attributes before he got to the interesting parts. She still insisted on a proper atmosphere during the day. At night, she was a different creature. "We were talking about my brother."

"Go ahead."

"When we were growing up, Marty was always in trouble. He got in fights and stole things. It almost seemed that he preferred lies to the truth. And he was a huge tease."

"Did he steal your Barbie dolls?"

"Worse. He hid my books before I was done reading them."

He imagined her as an adorable little girl with curly black hair and incredible aquamarine eyes. "I bet you were a shy kid."

Her eyebrows arched. "We aren't talking about me."

He couldn't resist teasing. "With your cute little nose always buried in a book."

"After I was adopted," she continued, "I lost touch with Marty. We didn't go to the same schools. I hardly ever saw him."

"Did you miss him?"

"Sometimes." She exhaled a ragged sigh. "I can't help wondering what would have happened if Marty had been the one to be adopted. If he'd been with caring, nurturing parents, he might have turned out better."

Her insistence on talking about her brother made him think that there was more to this story—something more pertinent to her life right now. "Where's Marty now?"

"In jail."

"I'm sorry, Madeline."

"That isn't the worst part." Her slender fingers knotted together. "Marty came to me a couple of weeks ago, needing money. I couldn't refuse. I gave him everything I had, even ran up my credit cards to the max."

Which explained why she'd turned up on his doorstep flat broke and desperate for a job. He had wondered about her circumstances, about how a supposedly well-organized, intelligent woman didn't have a savings account.

Trusting her ne'er-do-well brother might have been foolish, but Blake knew all about family loyalty. He rose from his chair and went toward her. "I understand."

She held up her hand, warding off his approach. "There's more I need to tell you."

What the hell was this about? "Go on."

"I knew Marty was up to something, even when he promised to pay me back with interest. He said that if the police ever came looking for him, I should keep my mouth shut." Her eyes filled with pain. "I swear to you, Blake. I swear. I never suspected that he was talking about a major crime."

"Not murder."

"No, thank God. I didn't know what Marty had done until I got here and saw it on the news from Boston. He's in jail because he's suspected of stealing diamonds worth seven hundred thousand dollars."

"You think he's guilty."

"I don't know. The diamonds still haven't been recovered, and I hope the police will find that someone else is responsible." She clenched her fingers again in an attitude that was almost like prayer. "He's my brother. How could he do this?"

Blake hated this situation. Unwittingly, he'd hired the sister of a major felon to work with his son, to teach Duncan. Damn it. What if Marty's partners in crime came after her? What if she'd brought another form of danger into his house?

"If you'd told me this when you arrived, I wouldn't have hired you."

"You almost didn't hire me," she reminded him. "When I first arrived here, I didn't know what my brother had done. Only that he was in trouble again. That's something I've had to live with since birth."

"Does he know you're here?"

"No. I haven't heard anything from him."

He believed her. Madeline was the most honest person he'd ever known. "I don't blame you for your brother's crime. I'm glad you're here, glad you're part of our family now."

When she stepped into his embrace and rested her head against his shoulder, he realized that this was the first time they'd touched outside the bedroom. Her nearness felt right to him. Part of the family. His family.

He inhaled the fragrance of her thick, curly hair and whispered, "You're a good person, Madeline. You just got caught up in a bad situation."

She swiped the corner of her eye. A relieved smile curved her lips and brightened her face. "Thank you, Blake, for understanding. Being with you and Duncan means everything to me."

Before her gratitude took on an uncomfortable weight, he changed the topic. Gesturing to the photos, he said, "What do you think?"

She leaned over the photos. "You don't have Helen Fisher. According to Lucy Tucker, Helen ought to be considered a suspect in her brother's murder."

Though Blake agreed that Helen's hate-filled attitude could turn violent, he didn't consider her a possibility. "Duncan was clear about one thing. The person who grabbed him was male. A bad man."

Madeline looked up at him. "And you don't have Joe Curtis."

"I didn't see him this afternoon." And he couldn't think of a good excuse to stop by the police station and snap photos. "But I have an idea of how I can get his mug shot."

She cocked her head to one side. "How?"

"I did a restoration project for a Washington, D.C., client who's a hotshot in Homeland Security. He's got access to photos from police departments, and he owes me a favor. He can fax it to me."

"Maybe he can do a background check on Joe Curtis.

Maybe there's something in his past with LAPD that would explain why Duncan had such a strong reaction to him."

"I'll make the call," Blake said. "Tomorrow, we'll do this photo array. Right now, he's too tired."

"He did so well at the T-ball game. Today was wonderful."

And tonight, Blake thought, would be even better.

WITH A clear conscience, Madeline prepared for bed. Telling Blake about Marty had been difficult, but his response had warmed her heart. He thought of her as family, as part of his life. She couldn't hope for more.

She'd barely had a chance to brush her hair when she heard the tap on her bedroom door. "Blake?"

Just like last night, he told her to come out. This time, she opened the door confidently. A trail of votive candles lit her way down the hall to his bed. As she followed the flickering lights, she paused and blew each one out.

Tonight, she noticed, the door to Duncan's room was closed. As soon as she entered Blake's room, he swept her into his arms for a long, deep kiss.

With her senses reeling, she leaned back in his arms and gazed at his oh-so-sexy smile. "Are you worried about leaving Duncan alone?"

"He agreed to have his door locked tonight. He'll be safe." He leaned close and kissed the tip of her nose. "Why did you blow the candles out?"

"Fire hazard," she said.

His low chuckle resonated inside his chest. "Safety first."

"I *am* a schoolteacher."

His hands slid down her back and cupped her bottom,

positioning her firmly against him. "It's a good thing that I never had a teacher as pretty as you. I wouldn't have learned a thing."

"I know your type." She reached up to run her fingers through his disheveled hair. "The second-grade boy who gives me love notes and shares half of his candy bar."

"I'm not the first to have a crush on the teacher."

"Actually," she said, "I was hoping there might be something you could teach me."

"About what?"

"You seem to be an expert in here." Boldly, she gestured toward the bed. In these intimate moments with Blake, her normal inhibitions evaporated like dew on a hot summer morning. "Teach me."

He needed no further encouragement. In seconds, he had her on the bed. Stretched out on his sheets, she experienced a crash course in sensuality. His expert touch aroused her in ways she'd never imagined possible. His kisses left her breathless. Gasping, she asked, "How on earth do you do that thing with your tongue?"

"First lesson," he murmured. "Don't analyze."

"But how will I learn if I don't ask questions?"

"Number two." He nibbled below her earlobe. "Accept the experience."

Trembling sensations raised goose bumps on her arms. "How many lessons are there?"

"Only one more." He straddled her thighs, looked directly into her eyes and said, "Enjoy."

"That," she said, "I can do."

Willingly, she gave herself over to a surging tide of pleasure as he fondled and nibbled and caressed. A clever student, she found her own creative ways of giving back to him. When he finally entered her, her level of excitement was such that she felt as if she might expire from an overdose of sheer ecstasy.

Afterward, she lay beside him on the bed, fully satisfied and blissful. The word *love* popped into her mind. Did she love him?

With a shake of her head on his pillow, she chased that idea away. For now, it was more than enough to make love…rather than *being* in love.

Chapter Eighteen

The next morning, Madeline woke early, still sorting out her emotions and wishing it were as easy as pulling petals from a daisy. *I love him…I love him not.* Not an easy decision.

Instead of pondering all the complications of their relationship, she decided it was time to completely erase her guilt about Marty. Talking to Blake had been the hard part. Now she needed to come clean with Alma.

As usual, the housekeeper sat at the kitchen table, already dressed and coiffed with the puffy blond hairdo that hadn't changed in twenty years. Madeline's typical procedure was to start off the day by wiping down the countertops and sweeping crumbs off the floor. Instead, she poured herself a mug of coffee and took the chair opposite Alma. "There's something I need to tell you."

Using the remote, Alma clicked off the small television she'd been watching. "It's about Marty, isn't it?"

She nodded. "He's gotten himself into a lot of trouble back in Boston."

"I saw it on the news. He stole seven hundred thousand dollars' worth of diamonds." She hoisted a penciled eyebrow. "And the loot still hasn't been recovered."

Madeline eyed her curiously. "You knew but you didn't say anything?"

"I didn't want to mess up this thing you've got going with Blake. You turned out okay, Madeline. I'm proud of you. Twenty-three kids passed through my home, and most of them are doing just fine. But you? You're special."

Though Alma's compliment had the ring of sincerity, Madeline didn't quite trust her. "You stay in touch with all your former fosters?"

"I do my best, hon. It doesn't take much to send a Christmas card or an occasional note."

"I remember those notes." Most of which related to a "great new project" that Alma was selling, like mail-order detergent, homemade jewelry or hypoallergenic makeup. Madeline had purchased some of these things, which undoubtedly kept her on Alma's list.

Her former foster mother had a mercenary side and generally put her own self-interest above all other concerns. But she wasn't a bad person.

"I never had any kids of my own." Her brassy voice softened with a sigh. "Sometimes I think that was a big mistake. I like kids."

"Even Duncan?"

"He's a dickens. But he's not mean, and he's got his father's good looks. Duncan can be as cute as a little angel."

Though this was the first time she'd heard Alma say anything nice about Duncan, the housekeeper was always gentle with Blake's son. The only household chore she took seriously was the preparation of Duncan's meals.

Alma continued, "If your fling with Blake goes anywhere, I want you to remember who's responsible for getting you this job."

Not quite ready to say thank you, Madeline asked, "Did you stay in contact with Marty?"

"I always liked your brother. He's a rogue. But such a handsome young man."

"You've seen him? Recently?"

In her fuzzy slippers, Alma shuffled to the coffee machine for a refill. "Marty always had your best interests at heart."

Madeline seriously doubted that. "Why do you think so?"

"Here's the thing. You weren't topmost in my mind when Blake started looking for a tutor. The real reason I got in touch with you was that Marty called me and said that you needed a job."

Her explanation sounded innocent. Perhaps too innocent. "Why didn't you tell me this before?"

"Must have slipped my mind."

Not likely. Alma had a reason for keeping her conversation with Marty a secret. She was covering something up. Like what? *Like his plan to steal the diamonds?*

That had to be the answer. Alma and Marty were working together. "Oh my God, you're his accomplice."

"Don't be silly, Madeline. I was here in Maine when Marty was robbing that safe."

Her statement was as good as a confession. "How do you know when he was committing the robbery?"

"Just guessing." Her shoulders twitched in another shrug.

"How do you know he robbed a safe?"

"Calm down." She returned to the table and sat. "Let's just take it easy, okay?"

Her eyes darted as if searching for a plausible lie, but it

was too late. Madeline already had a pretty good idea of what had happened. "You knew what Marty was planning."

"I tried to talk him out of it. I warned him. Told him that he'd probably get caught. And he did, didn't he?"

Madeline was all too familiar with her brother's machinations and his persuasive skills. "He talked to you because he wanted something. What was it?"

"He asked me to take care of you. He wanted you to get out of town and asked me if I could invite you to stay with me. Since Blake was already looking for a tutor, it seemed like a perfect fit."

"What did you ask for in return? What was your payoff?"

"He promised that he'd make it worth my while. After the heat died down in Boston, he was going to come up here and join us."

"Why?"

Her gaze sharpened. "In the last call I had from Marty, he said the diamonds were with you."

Shocked, Madeline sat back in her chair. "With me?"

"At first, I thought you knew about the jewels, that you were hiding them." Her tongue slid across her lower lip as if tasting the sweetness of promised wealth. "If I found them, I figured that I'd get a reward."

"You searched my things."

"I'm not proud of myself," Alma admitted. "I should have known that you'd never do anything illegal. You've always been a good girl."

"It was you." Incredulous, Madeline glared. "You were the one who kept sneaking into my room and going through my stuff."

"But no harm done. Now that I've explained, we can

forget about it. There's no need to tell Blake." She tried a smile. "Am I right?"

Anger surged through Madeline, driving her to her feet. "What about the basement? Did you lock me and Duncan in the dark basement so you could search?"

"I needed time to go through all your things."

"How could you?"

"I wasn't thinking straight." Alma stood on the opposite side of the table. She was at least six inches shorter than Madeline. "I didn't plan to trap you down there. But when I saw you both go into the basement, I took advantage of the situation."

"I was scared half to death. Duncan could have been traumatized."

Alma spread her small hands, holding out an invisible olive branch. "I'm sorry. Truly, I'm sorry."

"Why should I believe you?"

"I'd never do anything to hurt that little boy. I might not be the best housekeeper in the world. Or the most upright, honest human being. But I like kids. I really do." Once again, her voice muted. "Poor little Duncan. He's had it rough. I want the best for him."

Though still furious, Madeline believed that voice, that tone as soothing as a lullaby. Though Alma pretended to be tough, she liked kids, wished she had some of her own. But that didn't excuse what she'd done. "What about Marty's accomplice? Is there somebody else coming after these jewels that I don't have?"

"No," Alma said simply. "Marty planned the heist by himself. He'd been working construction at the home of these rich people and somehow got the combination to their safe. He was working alone."

"You believe him?"

"Your brother has never lied to me."

Unlike the way he'd treated her. Marty had looked her straight in the eye and told one lie after another. He'd used her to get what he wanted, what he needed.

"There's one lie," Madeline said. "He never gave the jewels to me."

"I guess not." The air went out of her, and she sank back into her chair. "Are you going to tell Blake?"

"I haven't decided," Madeline said. "But I promise you this. From now on, you're washing the dishes and scrubbing the floors. You're going to do the job you were hired for."

Unable to stand being in the kitchen with Alma for one more second, she stalked down the hallway to the front door and went outside. A misty rain was falling. Through the hazy sky, the morning light spread lightly on the treetops and the grassy yard. From the cliff beyond the forest, she heard the echo of the surf pounding against the rocky shore.

Madeline should have been relieved to know that Alma had been the one who pawed through her things when she first arrived at the Manor. No other person had been entering the house through the secret passageway. It was only Alma. A confused and deceptive woman. But not a murderer.

Through the mist, she saw a shadow moving through the trees. A glimpse of darkness.

And Madeline knew the danger was not yet over.

THE RAINY WEATHER meant Blake's construction crew wouldn't be working today, and he was glad for the break.

He needed some creative time for himself to complete the project he'd been working on in the upstairs front bedroom. He stepped back from the wall mural he'd just completed. A damn fine job, if he said so himself.

The four-poster bed was made, and the curtains were hung. Only a few more details needed to be added. Though the bold color in this design scheme didn't match the American Federalist decor in the rest of the house, he knew that Madeline would love this room.

The only other project on his schedule for the day was the photo array, and he was prepared. His former client at Homeland Security had already faxed a mug shot for Joe Curtis and promised to check further into Curtis's background with LAPD.

He and Madeline planned the photo array for midafternoon—about an hour from now. If Duncan was upset by what he saw or what he sensed, they'd have plenty of time to get him calmed down before bed.

As he adjusted the red velvet curtains, Blake looked through the window and saw headlights cutting through the steady rain. A jolt of tension went down his spine. Who the hell was coming here? He had a bad feeling about this unscheduled visitor.

Leaving the bedroom, he went downstairs and opened the door for Perry Wells. Stepping inside, the mayor brushed droplets from the sleeves of his trench coat. He took off his rain hat and dragged his fingers through his salt-and-pepper hair. The man looked like hell. His complexion was pasty white. "That's a nasty little storm," he said. "I trust you're all well."

"The heating system in the Manor leaves a lot to be desired," Blake said. "The furnace is relatively new, but a lot of ducts are clogged, and the windows aren't properly sealed."

"Your renovations will take care of those problems."

"Hope so." He didn't really think Mayor Wells had come here for an update on the progress of the restoration. "What can I do for you, Perry?"

"You mentioned that you might be interested in purchasing a property I own. I'm willing to drop my asking price to expedite the deal."

"But I haven't even looked at the house."

"We could go right now," he offered.

Blake was tempted. His experience in the housing market told him that the best bargains came when the seller was desperate. And that word described everything about Perry. Desperate.

As a businessman, he ought to take advantage. But he'd be a rotten human being if he exploited this man's fear. "Let me take your coat, Perry. We need to talk."

When Blake entered his office, he turned on the overhead light. On a sunny day, the windows provided enough illumination to see clearly. Today was gray and murky.

He sat behind his desk. "Tell me why you're so anxious to get rid of this property."

"There's nothing wrong with the house. It's a fine little place." Instead of sitting, he paced behind the chair. "I need to improve my cash flow. Immediately."

"To hire a lawyer?" Blake cut to the chase. There was no point in dancing around the issue. "You'll need an experienced attorney to defend you if you're charged with murder."

"What have you heard?"

"I know the evidence against you is mounting."

He braced both hands on the back of the chair opposite Blake's desk. His fingers clenched, white-knuckled. "The police are at my house right now, executing a search warrant."

"What are they going to find?"

"Documents." He peered at Blake through red-rimmed eyes. "Teddy and I had a business arrangement. He needed political favors, and I complied with his wishes. I'm sure you understand. You're a man of the world, a businessman. Sometimes it's necessary to make a deal with the devil."

"What kind of deal?"

"Rebuilding Raven's Cliff after the hurricane has been expensive. Our coffers ran dry months ago. That's when Teddy Fisher stepped up with a supposedly philanthropic offer to help repair the damages. A supposedly generous offer." His tone was bitter. "In exchange for this philanthropy, he asked me to keep the inspectors away from his lab and to issue necessary permits for the purchase of raw materials. It all seemed innocent enough. Just a matter of expediency."

"Then you learned that Teddy's experiments caused the genetically mutated fish, which, in turn, started the epidemic."

"People died." He circled the chair and sat heavily. "With better oversight, those experiments would never have gone forward. I blame myself. For each and every one of those tragic deaths, I blame myself."

His shoulders bowed under the burden of his guilt. Though the mayor's political skills undoubtedly included the ability to look contrite, he wasn't faking this emotion. His grief was too raw.

Blake almost felt sorry for him. Almost. "Why didn't you expose Teddy?"

"I should have. I'm sorry. So terribly sorry."

It was all too easy for politicians to make their heartfelt apologies and throw themselves on the mercy of public opinion. "Don't look to me for forgiveness," Blake said. "Even after you knew what Teddy was doing, you continued to grant him favors. You worked your political magic and made it possible for him to purchase the Manor and to hire me."

"I stand behind that decision." He straightened in the chair. "Teddy promised to restore the lighthouse. To end the curse."

"Come on, Perry. You're a man of the world. You don't believe in superstitions." Blake was losing sympathy fast. "You couldn't turn Teddy over to the police because it made you look bad. You went along with him to save your own hide."

"That's not the only reason."

Perry's face twisted as if he were in physical pain, but Blake wasn't buying these crocodile tears. The mayor had sold his soul to the devilish Teddy Fisher, and now he was reaping the consequences. "Did you know about the lab Teddy set up in the caves? It's likely he was continuing his experiments."

"I didn't know."

"But maybe you figured it out." Blake sensed that he might be treading on dangerous ground. As he continued to talk, he unlocked his desk. His gun was in the lower left drawer within easy reach. "Maybe you knew exactly what Teddy had in mind, and you couldn't let him do it again. You couldn't let other innocent people die."

Perry rose to his feet. "You've got it all wrong."

"Do I?" Blake eased the lower drawer open. If he needed

the gun it was within reach. "I think you finally realized that the only way you could stop Teddy was to kill him."

Perry slammed his fist down hard on the desktop. "I'm not a murderer. Teddy deserved to die, but I couldn't do it. I couldn't."

"Why not?"

"Camille."

His daughter? What did any of this have to do with his daughter? "She's dead, Perry."

"Her body was never found. Teddy said she'd survived. He knew where she was. If I didn't help him, I'd never see Camille again."

Surprised, Blake jolted back in his chair. He sure as hell hadn't seen this coming. "Did you tell the police?"

"I was afraid." He trembled. "If there was any chance that Camille was still alive…"

Blake doubted that possibility. From what he'd heard, the whole town had witnessed Camille's death. More likely, Teddy had been clever enough to use the one threat that he knew would be effective in tying Perry's hands. His love for his daughter.

From down the hallway, he heard voices and the clamor of footsteps. Detective Lagios entered the study.

After a nod to Blake, he confronted the mayor and said, "Perry Wells, you're under arrest for the murder of Teddy Fisher. You have the right to remain silent…"

Chapter Nineteen

"Rain, rain, go away. Come again another day." Duncan stared through the window in the family room. He wanted to be outside. "Rain, rain, go away…"

"Hey, buddy." His daddy picked him up off his feet and spun around in a circle. "Madeline and I have a new game for you."

"Don't want a new game. I want baseball."

"We can't do that in the house. There's not enough room for the bases."

"Ninety feet from home to first." Duncan shook his head. "Not enough room."

Daddy set him down, and they went to the table where he did art projects. This morning, he'd drawn a picture of a baseball diamond and his new friend Annie. She was funny. Some of the other kids called her Annie Banana, but he didn't.

"Here's what I want you to do," Daddy said. "I want you to try to remember the man who grabbed you on the cliff."

"Geez Louise." He slapped his forehead the way he'd seen kids do at T-ball. "I told you before, Daddy. I didn't see his face."

"I know. But maybe if we show you some pictures, you'll remember."

"How many pictures?"

"Seven," Madeline said. "You take a look, then tell us if you remember anything. Let's start with this one."

She set a picture down on the table.

"That's Coach Grant." He whisked the picture off the table onto the floor. "Ready for number two."

Two, three and four were men he had seen. But they didn't mean anything. He shoved their pictures away. Number five was different. He looked real close with his nose right down by the paper. "This man came to our house today. And he left with the policeman."

He shoved the picture aside, but his Daddy put it back in front of him. "I want you to pay attention, Duncan. Is this the man from the cliff?"

"No." This game was dumb. He didn't want to play anymore. "Number six. Number six."

Madeline slid another piece of paper onto the table. It was only a picture. But kind of scary. He didn't want to touch it. "He's a fisherman."

His face was not very nice. He looked dirty. At the same time, he made Duncan think about Temperance. She could tell him if this man meant danger. Under his breath, he hummed, "She sells seashells by the…"

"Duncan?" Daddy touched his arm. "Is this the man?"

"No, no, no." With the tip of his finger, he pushed the picture away. "Number seven."

A mean face stared up at him from the table. "A bad man. He's very bad."

"Is he the one?"

In the back of his head, he heard a loud thud. A hammer. "He hurts people. Sharks eat little kids. Don't go near the seashore."

He saw big waves splash on the rocks. *Danger.* He needed to get away.

"It's okay, buddy." Daddy patted his back. "Did this man grab you?"

"Upstairs." He nodded. "In my bedroom."

Danger. He jumped off his chair and ran toward the kitchen. Alma was standing in front of him. He ran right into her.

She held him so he wouldn't fall down. She hugged him, and he felt warm inside. She didn't say anything, but he knew what she was thinking.

He patted her cheek. "I can't be your little boy, Alma. I already have a mommy."

"I know."

He liked her puffy hair. "We can be friends."

"I'd like that, Duncan." He stepped away from her and turned around. Daddy was right behind him. "We're all friends."

"You did good," Daddy said.

Duncan raised his hand. "High five."

There was only one person in this room who he hadn't hugged. Madeline. He could tell that she felt left out, and that made him sad.

He marched over to her, and she squatted down so her eyes were even with his. Pretty eyes.

He kissed her forehead above her glasses. She smelled like flowers. "I like you best of all."

"Thank you, Duncan."

He hugged her for a long time. She was cozy. They would be friends forever and ever and ever and ever.

But he felt something else. A shiver. He stepped back. "You must be very careful."

"I will."

"Danger, Madeline. Danger."

LATER THAT NIGHT while Blake was putting Duncan to bed, Madeline sat behind his desk in his studio. She still felt a pleasant glow from when Duncan had hugged her. His sweet little kiss on her forehead ranked as one of the most precious moments in her life. She had been waiting for such a long time for him to allow her to touch him and cuddle him. Now, she truly felt like a member of the family.

Yet, Duncan's warning about danger wasn't a message she wanted to hear. Flipping through their collection of mug shots, she tried to decide which of these men presented a threat. Duncan hadn't sensed any danger from his T-ball coach. He'd paused on the photo of Perry Wells. Something about Perry worried him but didn't frighten him.

The next photo was Lucy's boyfriend, Alex Gibson—a handsome, rugged man. When Duncan had looked at his face, he seemed disturbed then started humming the seashell song. In a way, that made sense because Alex was a fisherman. At the T-ball game, Alex had argued with Helen Fisher. He wanted the lighthouse to be rebuilt so the curse would be ended. A superstitious man. But was he dangerous?

Certainly not as scary as Joe Curtis. Duncan's negative reaction to the cop was unmistakably clear. Perhaps Curtis hadn't touched the boy when he stood on the cliffs, but he seemed to represent the greatest danger. She hadn't seen him since she'd warned him off with a bluff. Was that enough to keep him away from the Manor?

When Blake entered the studio, he came around the

desk and lightly kissed her cheek. "Let's go upstairs. I have something to show you."

A combination of instinct and passion told her to follow him up the stairs to the bedroom. To follow anywhere he wanted to go. But she couldn't let go of her suspicions. Holding up the photo of Curtis, she said, "This is the bad guy. Duncan thought so."

"Duncan didn't directly identify Curtis as the man who grabbed him." He unfastened the clip holding her hair up in a high ponytail. Her thick, heavy curls cascaded around her shoulders. "Let it go, Madeline. There's nothing we can do."

She looked away from him, remembering the big, muscle-bound cop aiming at her with his cocked finger. "I can't forget. He's dangerous."

"But he's not the one under arrest." He pulled out the photo of Perry Wells. "Duncan might have a psychic feeling. And you might have a hunch. But Lagios needed evidence to take the mayor into custody."

"What kind of evidence?" she asked.

"He practically confessed to me, and there are other people he could have talked to. Plus, there are the facts— Perry admitted to being the last person to see Teddy alive. The police found incriminating papers at his house."

What if the police were wrong? It wouldn't be the first time an innocent man had been accused of murder. "Wasn't your Homeland Security contact going to send you more information about Curtis?"

He went around the desk to the fax machine near the door and picked up a single sheet of paper. For a moment, Blake read in silence. "Damn."

"What is it?"

"The photograph of Joe Curtis on file with the Raven's

Cliff police department doesn't match the records from the LAPD. He faked his credentials."

Though wary, she asked, "Who is he?"

"My contact at Homeland Security ran his real photo through a system designed to recognize facial features. He found a match with a man who's on the official terrorist watch list. He works for an organization called the GFF, Global Freedom Front." When he met her gaze, his jaw was tense. "The man we know as Joe Curtis is an assassin."

Icy dread shivered down her spine as she thought of an assassin walking among them, passing as a policeman, someone to be trusted and accepted. A perfect disguise. "What should we do?"

"It's out of our hands. Homeland Security already got in touch with the local cops. And they're sending federal agents." He reached for the phone. "I'm calling Lagios."

She fidgeted behind the desk while Blake made his phone call. A professional assassin? It didn't make sense. What was a terrorist doing in Raven's Cliff? What could possibly have drawn him to this quiet little fishing village? Madeline was fairly sure that he didn't come here for the ambience or the trinkets.

Blake hung up the phone and turned to her. From his worried expression, she deduced that he didn't have good news. "Curtis is still at large."

"Maybe he's making a run for it," she said hopefully. "I hope he's running fast and far away from us."

"For now, Lagios is keeping his identity a secret, hoping they can find him before he bolts."

"So Curtis doesn't know the police are after him."

"Not yet."

"What if he comes here?"

Blake nodded. "I mentioned that possibility to Lagios, and he promised to send a couple of cops out here to keep an eye on things."

She shook her head. "I can't believe this is happening."

"It's all under control."

As she leaned her cheek against his shoulder, Madeline did her best to believe him. The danger would pass, and they'd be free from fear. Soon, she hoped. "Why would a terrorist come to Raven's Cliff?"

"Fisher Labs," he murmured. "That seems to be the only link with this little town and the wider world. Fisher Labs and Teddy's research."

"That formula he created."

"A nutrient that mutated the fish and caused an epidemic," Blake said. "In the hands of terrorists, Teddy's formula could cause a global outbreak."

That outcome was too horrifying to imagine. Though she nuzzled more tightly in his arms, her stomach plummeted. "It feels like I'm on a roller coaster. Every time I start feeling happy, I go into a tailspin."

"Come upstairs with me, Madeline. I have something to show you that will make you feel better."

The only thing to soothe her jangled nerves would be to see Joe Curtis being dragged off in handcuffs. But she appreciated Blake's effort.

At the top of the staircase, he led her past Duncan's room where the door was carefully locked. He stopped outside the forbidden room where he'd been working for the past couple of days.

"Your secret project," she said.

"Curious?"

"A bit."

He pushed open the door and turned on the light. "I call it the Madeline Room."

The red velvet curtains were the first thing to catch her eye. Then the antique white four-poster, also with red bed-covers. "It's red, like my dress."

"Scarlet is your color."

Beneath the crown moldings, an incredible mural decorated the wall nearest the closet. The style matched the other formal landscape paintings in the house, paying great attention to detail. But the colors for this painting were vivid—the strong blues and greens of a forest splashed with brilliant yellow and purple wildflowers. In their midst stood a woman in a crimson dress with long black hair flowing down her back. "Is that me?"

"It's why I call it the Madeline Room."

"You painted this?"

He shrugged. "I studied art before I got into architecture."

The breadth of his talent awed and amazed her. Reaching toward the wall, she traced the branches of the trees and each petal of the flowers. His painting made her feel as beautiful as a work of art. "This is the best present anyone has ever given me."

Stepping up behind her, he wrapped his arms around her waist. "Nothing I give you could ever equal what you've done for me. And for Duncan."

She rested in his embrace, almost forgetting the danger that swirled around them. An assassin. A terrorist. She hoped their police guards would get here soon.

Turning, she kissed his cheek and smiled. "Much as I adore being in your arms, I want to take a closer look at the Madeline Room."

Slowly, she paced around the perimeter, exploring the

exquisite details. All of the furniture was antique white, painted with a delicate primrose pattern that looked charmingly old-fashioned and very familiar.

"My ficus." She recognized the design. "This is the same design that's on the pot holding my ficus."

"Your family heirloom."

"Not that it's worth anything, but it's special to me. Let's bring it in here."

"My thought exactly."

They hurried down the hall, treading quietly so they wouldn't wake Duncan. Blake lifted the plant in its pretty container and carried it.

Anxious to see this finishing touch, she crowded through the door beside him. She bumped his elbow. He tripped. Before either of them could catch their balance, the urn holding the ficus crashed to the floor.

The primrose pottery broke into shards.

She knelt and picked one up. "It's lucky you painted a duplicate so I won't forget what this looked like."

"Sorry," he said. "This urn was important to you."

"A reminder of the past." Her regrets were minimal. The time had come to forget about her childhood in foster care—to break with her lingering sadness and repression. "I'd rather think about the future."

Picking through the shards and dirt, Blake found a zippered satchel. "What's this?"

"I have no idea."

He unfastened the zipper and poured a glittering array of cut diamonds into his hand. The sparkle took her breath away. Seven hundred thousand dollars' worth of jewels.

Marty must have stashed them in the pot, knowing that she'd never leave it behind.

When she reached toward the shimmering jewels, Blake pulled his hand back. His hazel eyes darkened with rage. "How could you do this to me? To Duncan?"

"Do what?"

"I trusted you. I accepted your teary-eyed confession about how your black-sheep brother used you."

"It was the truth."

"I'm not naive, Madeline. I can see what you are. Your brother's accomplice. You came here to hide out from the Boston police."

Shocked by his accusation, she sat back on her heels. "I knew nothing about this."

"You showed up here with nothing but your clothes, a couple of boxes and this ficus. Don't expect me to believe that was a coincidence."

"I didn't know. Really, Blake. Marty told Alma that the jewels were with me, but I had no—"

"Alma was in on this?"

He stood abruptly. His passion for her had turned to cold rage—the same outraged, overprotective fury she'd seen in him when she first arrived at the Manor. From experience, she knew there was no reasoning with him when he was in this mood. "Think what you want."

"I'll be turning this loot over to the police as soon as they get here. You might want to work on your story."

Unfolding herself from the floor, she stood tall. "I'll tell the truth."

"That your brother stole the jewels and they just happened to end up in your possession?" He scoffed. "I want you out of here. Tomorrow morning. And Alma, too."

He strode from the room, leaving her alone.

How could he be so quick to judge? Yes, the circumstances looked bad, but he ought to know by now that she wasn't a bad person.

A sob caught in her throat as she looked at the mural he'd painted for her. Another dip on the emotional roller coaster. With Blake, she experienced the highest highs and the most abject lows.

She trudged down the hall to her bedroom and closed the door. Pain washed over her. And remorse. Even though she hadn't done anything wrong, she felt guilty.

Perhaps it was better to find out now that his affections were fickle. A simple twist of fate had transformed Blake from a romantic lover into a tyrant. How could she have ever thought she was in love with him?

Then she heard the tap on her door.

He'd changed his mind.

He was coming to apologize.

She threw open the door. A cloth covered her mouth. She couldn't breathe. Everything went black.

Chapter Twenty

Behind the closed door of his studio office, Blake stared through the window into the night. Raindrops rattled against the windowpanes in a furious staccato. How could he have been so wrong about Madeline? He had believed her, trusted her. Maybe even loved her.

And she had used him. Used his home as a hideout. Everything about her was a lie. Her sweetness. Her common sense. Her passion. All lies.

Anger surged through him. How could she have done this to him? He'd opened his heart to Madeline. For the first time since Kathleen's death, he felt like there was a reason to get out of bed in the morning. With Madeline, he'd found hope—a reason to start looking forward instead of living in the past. She'd changed him…and betrayed him.

How could she have done this to Duncan? His son would be brokenhearted when she left. Somehow, Blake had to find a way to explain to Duncan that his beloved teacher was nothing but a thief, a criminal. It didn't seem possible.

But it was true.

Returning to his desk, he unzipped the pouch and spilled the diamonds across the surface. Here was proof, undeniable proof.

Where the hell were those cops Lagios promised to send? As soon as they got here, Blake intended to turn over the diamonds and point them toward Madeline. They could take her into custody, ship her back to Boston. She'd get what she deserved.

Pain cut through his anger. How could he do this to her? How could he stand by and watch while she was arrested, marched off in handcuffs? Not Madeline. Not the woman he loved. He wanted to shelter and protect her, wanted a future with her.

That hope was dead.

He gathered the gems in his hand. As he closed his fist, a strange heat shot up his arm, igniting a stream of fire that pulsed through his veins and arteries. He was consumed by sensation. Inside his rib cage, his heart pounded. Each heavy beat echoed louder than the last.

What was happening to him? He had to fight. Be strong. But he couldn't resist.

His knees folded and he dropped into his desk chair, too weak to stand. The room began to whirl. The light from his desk lamp blurred into jagged lightning bolts outside the window. Spinning faster and faster, he couldn't breathe.

He closed his eyes. Everything went still, as if he'd entered the eye of a hurricane. He was floating, detached, unaware of bodily sensation.

Behind his eyelids, he saw a scene being played out. It was unreal, dreamlike. Yet every detail came through with crystal clarity. A clock on the wall. A purse on the table. Madeline's purse. A man he didn't recognize held the pouch. As if from far away, he heard Madeline's voice. "Marty, is that you?"

The stranger replied, "Be right there, sis."

He dug into the dirt beside the ficus, buried the pouch. Blake could hear his thoughts. *She'll never leave this pot behind. I'll get the stones later.*

In a jolt, Blake returned to his studio. Everything was exactly as it had been. The rain still slashed at the window. The desk lamp shone on the gems.

There was no rational explanation for what had just occurred, but he knew that he had seen the truth. He'd seen the past. Marty had hidden the gems without telling Madeline.

Blake had experienced a vision. The realization stunned him. Just like his son, he'd been thrown into an altered state of consciousness. All these years, he'd denied the possibility of psychic awareness. He hadn't understood why Duncan wore gloves to ward off these feelings.

Now he knew. He and his son were alike. Hypersensitive. They saw things that other people didn't know about.

Slowly, Blake rose from his chair. His legs were still weak, but his heartbeat had steadied. His breathing was normal. He felt a lightness—a purity of thought he'd never known.

Madeline was innocent. She'd been duped by her conniving brother.

Blake never should have doubted her, should have trusted the inherent instinct that told him she was a good person, worthy of trust, worthy of love.

At the edge of his desk, he saw the barrette she used to clip her hair into a high ponytail. Earlier tonight, he'd unfastened the tortoiseshell barrette, allowing her curly black hair to cascade. *I'm sorry, Madeline.*

He picked it up. In an instant, his head was spinning. Another vision crashed into his mind.

He felt her terror. She was unable to move. Her wrists and ankles were bound with rope.

Through her eyes, he saw the dark walls of the cave.

Through her ears, he heard the roaring surf.

A necklace of shells lay on the sand beside her.

She had only minutes left before that necklace was placed around her neck and tightened, choking off her breath.

LYING ON her back on the cold wet sand, Madeline blinked slowly. The insides of her eyelids felt scratchy and crusted as if she'd been crying for days. She could barely see. Her glasses were gone. But she knew where she was. The caves. She could smell the ocean and hear the waves. Must be close to the mouth of the cave.

Another blink. Her vision cleared. The dim light of an electric torch glowed against the stone walls.

How had she gotten here? She struggled to sit up but couldn't. *I can't move.* Her lungs ached as if a huge, heavy hand pressed down upon her chest.

Concentrating, she tried to lift her arm. Only a slight twitch. Looking down, she saw that her wrists were tied together. She had to get up. Had to get away.

Another effort. Nothing. She was paralyzed.

"You're awake."

The face of Joe Curtis swam into focus. She struggled to speak but could only manage a groan.

"It would have been better," he said, "if you'd stayed unconscious."

Why? What was he going to do?

"When they autopsy your body, they'll find the same

mix of drugs that were in the other victims. I've got all the details right." His heavy shoulders shrugged. A casual gesture. "That's the good thing about using a cop's identity. I know the details of the Seaside Strangler's procedure. There's no way I'll be blamed for this murder."

He didn't know his cover had been blown. He didn't know that Lagios and the rest of the Raven's Cliff police force were searching for him.

If she'd been able to speak, she could have told him. There was no need to murder her. His time would be better spent running away.

He unfastened the rope binding her ankles. "I knew you were bluffing about being psychic. But that kid? When he looked at me, it was like he saw inside. I can't take the chance that he told you. Did he?"

He looked into her eyes. There was no way she could respond.

"Doesn't matter," he said. "After you're out of the way, it won't be hard to get to the kid. Maybe he'll have a tragic fall from the cliffs."

Desperately, she tried to shake her head, to signal to Curtis that he didn't need to go after Duncan.

She managed a tiny movement. The resulting pain caused her to wince. It was as though her entire body had fallen asleep. She had to wake up.

He stood, looming over her. "Your legs are untied. Go ahead. Try to run."

She exerted a fierce effort. Couldn't move. Not an inch. Her toes tingled painfully, like a thousand needles being stabbed into her feet.

Sensation was returning to her body. If she could feel, she could move. And she had to get away, had to protect Duncan.

"Nothing personal," Curtis said as he untied her hands. "But I have to strip you. The Strangler dresses his victims in white. Like virgins. That's not you. Is it, Madeline?"

She tried to protest but could only make an unintelligible noise.

"I know about you and Blake," he said. "I've been keeping an eye on the Manor. It's easy to slip in and out through an unlocked window. Tonight, I went through that secret passage. Pretty nifty."

He unbuttoned her shirt.

Hoping to distract him, she managed to blurt a single word. "Teddy."

"You want to know if I killed Teddy?" Roughly, he pushed the fabric off her shoulders. "Hell, yes. The little traitor deserved to die. He was supposed to be manufacturing that fish nutrient, the one that caused the epidemic. Hell of a thing, huh? That prissy little scientist was trying to cure world hunger. Instead, he came up with an efficient weapon for biological warfare. In the right hands—our hands—that weapon can control the world."

As he lifted her torso and took off her shirt, the prickling beneath her skin became an aching throb. A shudder went through her.

He dropped her back onto the sand. There was nothing sexual about the way he removed her clothing. Stripping her was just part of his job.

"Assassin," she said.

He eyed her curiously. "Did you say assassin?"

She blinked her eyes as if to nod.

"You're wrong about that, lady. I believe in what I'm doing. I'm a soldier for the cause."

Madeline knew she'd struck a chord. Forcing the breath through her lips, she repeated the word. "Assassin."

"You don't get it. The people I work for paid hundreds of thousands of dollars to Teddy Fisher. He was supposed to deliver. All of a sudden, he grew a conscience. He didn't want us to poison the world's food supply. Not that we were going to kill everybody."

"Why?"

"Some populations would have to go. Those who are a drain on the world's resources. The poor. The sick." Another shrug. "For most of those people, death is a welcome cure."

In his voice, she heard the insane logic of a fanatic. Joe Curtis was a true believer. What was the name of his group? Global Freedom Front. GFF.

"When I saw that Teddy had destroyed every speck of the nutrient, I tried to get him to tell me the formula, tried to beat it out of him with a hammer. He wouldn't talk."

In the end, she thought, Teddy Fisher had been a hero. He'd stood up to Joe Curtis. And he'd died in the effort.

She couldn't allow that same fate to befall her. She had to find the strength to move.

Efficiently, Curtis unbuttoned her jeans and tugged the wet fabric down her legs.

Sprawled on the sand in her bra and panties, she'd never been more vulnerable. Or more determined. She wasn't going to die. Not here. Not now.

She had to survive. All her life, she'd kept quiet, never stood up for herself. She hid behind her glasses, faded into the background like a quiet little wallflower. Not anymore. She was a woman who could wear a red dress. A fighter.

She wouldn't give up. *It's not my time to die.* She had

to live, to convince Blake of her innocence. She would have a life with him. And with Duncan.

Clumsily, Curtis pulled the flowing white gown over her head and down her body. The muscles in her shoulder tightened.

With every second that passed, she grew stronger. Her hand flexed. She made a fist.

ON THE BEACH, Blake saw the glow from the mouth of the cave. He knew Madeline was in there. *He knew.* His senses were heightened as never before.

Though he could have waited until the cops arrived, he didn't have that much time. He'd grabbed his handgun, told Alma where he was headed and instructed her to send the reinforcements in this direction.

The rush of the surf against the rocky shore covered the sound of his footsteps as he approached. A small dinghy had been pulled onto the sand. A garland of flowers draped across the bow. A signature of the Seaside Strangler.

His heart wrenched when he saw Madeline lying on the sand in a white dress. The huge form of Joe Curtis leaned over her. He placed the seashell necklace around her throat.

No time left. Blake stepped around the edge of the cave and aimed his gun. He was only ten feet away from them. "Back off."

Curtis looked up. "Come to rescue your girlfriend?"

"Get away from her. I'll shoot."

"Here's your problem," Curtis said. "I could snap her neck in one second."

Not as fast as a bullet. Blake aimed at the center of his

chest. A massive target. "Give it up, Curtis. The cops are on the way. They know all about you and the GFF."

"What?"

"Information from Homeland Security. They identified you from the terrorist watch list."

Curtis stood. He yanked Madeline's limp body in front of him, using her as a shield. There was no chance for Blake to get a clear shot; he couldn't take the chance of hitting Madeline.

Curtis pulled his own gun. Before he could take aim, Madeline reacted. Her arm flung wildly. She stabbed at the big man's face, clawed his eyes.

With a cry, Curtis dropped her.

Blake fired. Three shots in rapid succession. At least two were direct hits.

Curtis staggered backward but didn't go down. He lowered his gun, aimed at Madeline.

Blake lunged. Before Curtis could pull the trigger, he tackled the big man and they both went down. Blood poured from the wounds in his chest, soaking them both.

Blake grabbed for his arm, slammed his wrist against the rocks. Curtis dropped the gun. For an instant, he lay still, and Blake thought he'd won.

Then Curtis surged to his feet. He threw Blake off him and staggered toward the dinghy. With the strength of a wounded beast, he shoved the boat into the surf. The waves churned against his calves.

Blake didn't give a damn if he got away. As long as Madeline was safe, he didn't care.

Curtis whirled. From inside his jacket, he pulled another gun. His huge hand shook as he took aim.

From behind his back, Blake heard a shot. Then another.

Curtis fell.

Blake turned and saw Madeline with his gun in her hand. Unsteady on her feet, she wavered.

He ran to her, enclosed her in his arms. She was ice-cold, nearly frozen. All the strength left her body as she collapsed against him.

From down the beach, he heard the police arriving.

"You're going to be all right," he said, as much to reassure himself as her. "It's over."

She murmured, "How did you find me?"

"I saw what was happening. It was a vision. Like Duncan has."

One corner of her mouth twitched as if she was trying to smile. "Runs in the family."

They were all a little bit psychic, a little bit crazy. "I had another vision about you and Marty and the diamonds. I know you were telling me the truth. I never should have doubted you."

Her luminous eyes gazed into his face. Her wet hair streamed across her forehead. The murderous shell necklace encircled her slender throat, a reminder of how close he'd come to losing her forever. "I love you, Madeline."

Her lips moved. She struggled to speak.

"Does this mean…" she gasped for breath "…that I'm not fired?"

She would never leave his side again. Madeline was the woman he meant to spend the rest of his life with.

SEVERAL DAYS LATER, Madeline stood in the yard outside the Manor and kept an eye on Duncan, who practiced hitting balls off the tee. His friend Annie would be here any minute for a playdate.

When Duncan connected with the ball for a solid hit, she waved to him and called out, "Good one."

Sunlight glittered on the huge sapphire in her engagement ring. The stone was spectacular, as blue as the sea. After Marty's crime, it didn't seem right to have a diamond. Poor Marty! After she'd turned in the stolen gems to the police and Alma gave her statement, he couldn't deny his guilt. With good behavior, he might be paroled from prison in eight years.

Though Alma had been charged for withholding evidence, she got off with a fine and probation, partly because both Blake and Madeline had testified as character witnesses. Alma was still with them in Raven's Cliff, doing her job as a housekeeper with renewed commitment.

Blake came through the front door and joined her. His arm fit so neatly around her waist. His kiss on her cheek was sweet and sexy at the same time.

"I just got off the phone with Perry Wells," he said.

Though Perry had been acquitted of murder charges when Joe Curtis had confessed to killing Teddy Fisher, the scandals hadn't gone away. Perry resigned his office in disgrace because of the sleazy agreements he'd made with Teddy. The only point that the good people of Raven's Cliff agreed upon was for renovations on Beacon Manor and the lighthouse to continue, using the money Teddy left in escrow.

"How's Perry?" she asked.

"Desperate for cash. He reduced the price on that house he owns. He wants to sell for about half of what it's worth."

"I like the house." More specifically, she liked the idea of having a residence in Raven's Cliff—a place they could always come back to after Blake's assignments took them to more exotic locales. "But it would be wrong to take advantage of Perry's distress."

He gave her a squeeze. "Don't worry, I'm not going to cheat anybody. Even though it would be a solid fiscal move."

"Good business," she said. "Bad karma."

"He started babbling about how there's a new lead on his daughter. He still thinks Camille is alive."

"Could be. After she blew off the cliff, her body was never found." Glancing toward the yard, she saw Duncan marching toward the trees.

"Hey, buddy," his father called out. "Don't go far."

"Okay." Duncan waved. "Only to the trees and back."

Blake whispered in her ear, "While Duncan is busy with his little friend, we could have a playdate of our own."

Delighted, she whispered back, "I'll meet you in the Madeline Room."

"Wear your red dress."

And nothing else but a lacy thong and a sapphire engagement ring. She grinned. Every day with Blake was a playdate.

Duncan looked back over his shoulder. Daddy was right next to Madeline, hugging her. He was always hugging her and kissing her. They were in love.

Duncan was glad. He liked Madeline.

Counting every step, he walked across the grass to the trees. Real quiet, he said, "She sells seashells."

"Here I am," Temperance said.

"I have another friend," he said. "I don't want you to be jealous. Her name is Annie."

"Very well," she said. "If ever you wish to speak with me, I shall be here."

He had a question for her. The big scary man with hammer hands was gone, but Duncan knew he wasn't the person who'd grabbed his shoulder on the cliff. "Is there more danger?"

"Not for you. Not for the moment."

"Who was the man on the cliff?"

She rolled her eyes. "I told you before. Nicholas Sterling, the lighthouse keeper's grandson. And he never meant to hurt you. He was pulling you away from the edge."

"But everybody says Nicholas Sterling is dead."

"Is he?"

He heard a car honk and heard it pull up in the driveway. Annie hopped out. He waved to her, then turned back. "Goodbye, Temperance."

She was already gone.

* * * * *

The danger still lurks in this quaint fishing village.
Next month, Elle James presents
UNDER SUSPICION, WITH CHILD, as
THE CURSE OF RAVEN'S CLIFF continues,
only in Harlequin Intrigue!

Romantic
SUSPENSE

**Sparked by Danger,
Fueled by Passion.**

Cindy Dees
Killer Affair

Seduction in the sand…and a killer on the beach.

Can-do girl Madeline Crummby is off to a remote
Fijian island to review an exclusive resort, and she hires
Tom Laruso, a burned-out bodyguard, to fly her there
in spite of an approaching hurricane. When their plane
crashes, they are trapped on an island with a serial killer
who stalks overaffectionate couples. When their false
attempts to lure out the killer turn all too real, Tom and
Madeline must risk their lives and their hearts….

**Look for the third installment
of this thrilling miniseries,
available August 2008
wherever books are sold.**

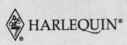
HARLEQUIN®

American ★ Romance®

CATHY MCDAVID
Cowboy Dad

THE STATE OF PARENTHOOD

Natalie Forrester's job at Bear Creek Ranch
is to make everyone welcome, which is an
easy task when it comes to Aaron Reyes—the
unwelcome cowboy and part-owner. His
tenderness toward Natalie's infant daughter
melts the single mother's heart. What's not
so easy to accept is that falling for him means
giving up her job, her family and the only
home she's ever known....

**Available August
wherever books are sold.**

LOVE, HOME & HAPPINESS

REQUEST YOUR FREE BOOKS!

2 FREE NOVELS PLUS 2 FREE GIFTS!

 HARLEQUIN®

INTRIGUE®

Breathtaking Romantic Suspense

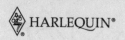